Criminal Justice

Jack N. Lawson

What They Are Saying About Criminal Justice

Prison Chaplain Stephen Travis is back after *Doing Time* in a new and thrilling prison sleuth adventure at the Fairborn Advancement Center for Men in North Carolina.

Everything starts rather innocuously, with the distant sound of mysterious gunshots which turn out to be the seed for an investigative melee into the disappearance of an inmate, playing out against the backdrop of a partially corrupt prison system—justice gone criminal.

The evolving plot features, besides the good-hearted, love-stricken, determined chaplain, Stephen Travis, several prison officials on both sides of the aisle—the good and the corrupt, and last but not least, doctoral student and animal researcher, Emily Webster. She turns a murderous crime tale into a most redeeming love story, which, never boring, lets us witness a loving courtship, witty-warm, enriched by, of all things, the digestive system of bovines and a rather surprising ending—legally wrong—ethically right.

The story plays during Jimmy Carter's presidency and it is highly actual and greatly relevant even, or especially, now during the time of "Black Lives Matter." It is brimming with autobiographical authenticity and peppered with factual and sobering information about the inadequacies of the US criminal justice system. Lawson, who wrote his doctoral thesis on "The Concept of Fate..." worked in younger years as a prison chaplain himself. He puts his considerable inside knowledge about our justice system and his personal life experience on full display, trying through his protagonists to take the blinders off "blind fate" and "blind justice."

Lawson's writing feels natural, fresh, surprisingly positive and almost playful. It does not feel provocative, but rather educative, like a good moral lecture that gives the discerning reader "contemplative" pause, opening our eyes to the many injustices and shortcomings that are systemically heaped on the downtrodden with seemingly no end in sight.

He seamlessly combines the good, the bad and the holy, by weaving an intricate web of greed and decency, fear and faith, corruption and love, into a compelling narrative, interceded with biblical wisdom and elevated by—what I especially like –a good dose of playful humor.

Criminal Justice is a suspenseful, mind opening, fun book to read, last, not least, with a hidden love message in plain sight: *tovim ha shana'im min ha'ekhad* —go figure!

—Bernhard Franz Josef Schiefer, Sieding-Ternitz, Austria

A criminal enterprise being run out of a prison? Chaplain Stephen Travis is back investigating a crime ring that's important enough to cause the death of an inmate to ensure his silence in *Criminal Justice*, a follow-up to author Jack Lawson's first novel, *Doing Time*.

Set in a men's transitional facility in Raleigh, North Carolina where inmates are prepared for their return to society, Chaplain Travis is one of the good guys, trying to find truth in a system that lacks much justice. Some of his fellow employees are corrupt, some are incompetent and some just burned out. But Travis knows that the life of an inmate matters—to his family, his friends inside and out, and to God. And he's determined to find that justice for inmate Walter Jackson, who was just days away from release before his murder.

Like any good character, Stephen Travis has a real human side, here represented by the interaction with his new girlfriend Emily, a grad student at N.C. State University. She helps him work out several elements of his investigation, but mostly keeps him centered when things start going south. She also has a surprise in her own personal history that helps connect her to the chaplain. The scenes between Stephen and Emily reflect a happy warmth that provides a welcome contrast to the problems happening inside the prison. And the chaplain's Jewish psychologist friend provides several instances of comic relief.

Criminal Justice feels real. The characters are real people trying to expose a crime of greed and manipulation. The relationships between characters black and white, good and bad, are real.

—Neill Caldwell
Long-time writer and newspaper editor
in North Carolina

Criminal Justice

Jack N. Lawson

Literary Fiction Novel

RESOURCE *Publications* · Eugene, Oregon

Resource Publications
A division of Wipf and Stock Publishers
199 W 8th Ave, Suite 3
Eugene, OR 97401

Criminal Justice
By Lawson, Jack N.
Copyright © 2020 by Lawson, Jack N. All rights reserved.
Softcover ISBN-13: 979-8-3852-6898-6
Hardcover ISBN-13: 979-8-3852-6899-3
eBook ISBN-13: 979-8-3852-6900-6
Publication date 10/31/2025
Previously published by Wings ePress, Inc., 2020

This edition is a scanned facsimile of the original edition published in 2020.

Dedication

This book is lovingly dedicated to Chris—wife, best friend and household muse!

Acknowledgements

The author would like to thank the following people for their help and support: my colleague, Rev. Steve Smith, who took a bullet to the head for the team—and lived to tell me about it! David "Big D" Wallace, long time friend and lawyer; Jeanne Smith, my gem of an editor who helps put my writing before a wider audience.

One

"What's this? The Fourth of July?"

Another inmate blurted out, "Fourth a' July my ass! Somebody been capped! That wasn't no firecracker."

Stephen Travis exited his windowless, airless office to see what the commotion was. "Hey, guys, I heard it too. What's going on?"

By then nearly everyone was moving toward the exercise yard behind the correctional center. Officer Fowler was already outside and seemed to be sniffing the warm, breezeless September air. Travis heard him mumble one word to himself, "Cordite." Fowler almost seemed surprised when he turned and saw the group of inmates behind him. Travis hadn't been the only one to hear Fowler speak. And Fowler wasn't the only military veteran in the crowd.

"Cordite! Yeah, see. Told you it wasn't no firecracker." Tyrone Mason seemed pleased with himself. "Better look for a body."

1

Travis joined James Fowler. "Can I help? Want me to check the grounds?"

Still speaking low and more to himself than to Travis, Fowler said, "I'm just wondering who loosed off those rounds. There were two shots." He turned and finally seemed to recognize Chaplain Travis. "Yeah, thanks man. You head over to the parking lot; I'm going up to the woods by the fence." Fowler turned and addressed the inmates. "Y'all get on back inside—see if anyone is missing." Fowler set out for the pines and the fence that bordered the Correctional Center for Women, which overlooked the Fairborn Advancement Center for Men.

This is an open prison, Stephen thought, as he walked the forty yards to the parking lot. *Who'd have a gun here?*

He had been used to the presence of various firearms at other high security units. But here? Stephen swung around the building through the lighted parking area. No bodies—or shell casings. Only five cars there, and one he didn't recognize, so he made a mental note of it. It was a souped-up 1967 Ford Fairlane, pale blue. "Who's on front desk tonight?" he asked himself while turning toward the front entrance. Skipping every other step, he mounted the stairs in three strides.

When he opened the front door, Melvin Strader was sitting at the desk looking bored and cleaning his nails with a pen knife. Without actually looking at Stephen, he asked laconically, "Wass'all the chatter back there?" He nodded his head in the direction of the lounge area, at the end of the narrow corridor.

"Didn't you hear anything?" queried Travis. "It sounded like two shots."

Strader slowly looked up, shaking his head and curling his lower lip. "Unh-unh. Maybe backfire. I dunno. I been watching the fight—Ali and Spinks." He jerked his gnarled thumb at the portable television on top of the file cabinet beside him. "Don't hear so well since Korea anyways. Why don't you go back and settle the fellows down?"

By the time Stephen was in the lounge area, the inmates, who were now referred to as "residents" at this pre-release unit, had already determined that one resident was indeed missing: Walter Jackson. "It's Jackson," they announced almost in unison, when they saw the chaplain. Travis simply nodded and then asked, "What about his stuff? Is everything there?"

"I saw him by his bunk not thirty minutes ago," threw in Delbert Moore, one of the few short-timers in this unit meant for long-timers who needed time to readjust to society after fifteen years or more behind bars. Delbert was also the best-educated person in the unit.

A cursory check by the men ascertained that all of Jackson's belongings were still in his locker. It was curious, a man soon to be released from prison—after God knew how many years—disappears and two apparent gunshots were heard. Yet both staff officers were there in the building and accounted for—and they were never meant to be armed. Stephen stood and shook his head. He reckoned it was simply another one of those strange things that happen within the weird world of prisons. He smiled as he remembered the "great prison break" which had happened several years before, when he was still a trainee chaplain at the women's prison up the hill. Twenty-seven women had cleared the fence. What a day that had been. And yet not a shot had been fired that day. Curious.

Travis went back into the office he shared with the unit's social worker, Lincoln Parker. Parker and he usually alternated evenings at the unit in order to have some privacy with the men who wanted to see them after their day's work—and especially after a fruitless day of trying to find a place to live. Jobs, as menial as they might be, were easier to come by than a place to call home. And they were the two requirements for the 'get out of jail' card every inmate needed before he could re-establish himself in the community. But some debts to American society can seemingly never be paid. Folk seemed happy enough to lock people up behind bars—but receive them back into society? That was another matter. Travis was glad the home plan was something he didn't have to deal with. And yet, he reminded himself, he did have to deal with the frustration and depression that overcame inmates in this stressful time just prior to release.

Stephen reflected that some of the men he worked with had been in prison since Travis was in primary school—when Eisenhower was still president! And now here we were five presidents later. He thought about how the world outside had continued to evolve even as the world within the prison walls and fences remained almost changeless, except for the staff and new inmates. The routines were immutable. Yet on the outside, cars changed, clothing and hair styles changed, the dollar wasn't worth half what it was in the 1950s. The world outside was almost like stepping into the "Twilight Zone" for most of these guys. Whenever Stephen took any of the men out on special parole—usually for funerals—they were like children in the house of horrors at the fair—turning at every new sound, amazed at the speed of modern cars, baffled by new roads that led to their homeplaces. It was a waking nightmare.

Stephen's reverie was broken by James Fowler standing in the doorway. "Busy?" Fowler asked laconically.

"Nah, come on in. Grab a chair."

Fowler rubbed his hand over his short Afro. Well, it was short for the current African-American hair styles, but as 'long' as the prison service would allow it. Fowler slowly lowered his strong, six-foot-three frame into the chair. He was something of a gentle giant. Ten years previously he had been an army medic in

Vietnam. As with so many veterans, the state correctional system let their military pensions and benefits continue to accrue. But then, a lot of former military men liked the para-military aspects of the correctional system: one had rank and a clear chain of command—even chaplains like Travis. There were regular weapons training sessions and riot control tactics at the North Carolina Justice Academy. The likes of Fowler and others in corrections laughed at the word "Justice" in the title. The first commandment everyone learned was to protect state property! Forget human life. No wonder Justice is always depicted as 'blind!'

Travis and the other chaplains had to go for the training occasionally—but not as often as the custodial staff. Stephen always felt guilty about having so many 'kill shots' when he was on the firing range. He was conflicted about wanting to do well—which was actually admired by a number of the guards—and the human silhouette at which he was aiming. He treated it as game that had to be played so he could get back to what he was called to do.

"Stephen," Fowler was stroking his mustache thoughtfully. "You notice anything odd about this business tonight?"

"You mean apart from two shots fired nearby the building and nobody in sight? And, oh yeah, Jackson is missing?"

"Yeah, all of that," mused Fowler, "but there's more."

"More?"

Fowler nodded, "Yeah. I was watching the Ali fight with most of the guys, except the two or three that were cleaning up in the kitchen. But when we heard the 'bangs' or shots, seven or eight men never got up from the TV. Doesn't that strike you as odd?"

Stephen let Fowler's words sink in for a few seconds. "Well, yes, I guess it does. Everything happened so fast, I didn't really think about it but...but now that you mention it, I did notice that not everybody crowded outside. It is a bit odd. When I came in the front door, Melvin was on the desk. He hadn't seemed to notice anything. Of course, he had the TV on and he is that bit hard of hearing. And when I got back to the lounge area, there were a bunch of guys still just sitting there."

Travis and Fowler sat in silence for a while. Then James slapped his thighs and stood up. "I've got a report to write. Gonna be short and weird. I mean, what am I gonna say?" Stephen simply shrugged as Fowler left.

Two

The next morning Stephen stood looking out his kitchen window, holding a steaming cup of tea under his nose, feeling the warmth rise around his face. He rubbed his chin, wondering whether he wanted to shave or grow a beard. But he knew his hair was already considered too long by Ralph Martin, head of the North Carolina Correctional Chaplaincy Services, so a beard would probably be too much. He hated shaving. Whatever he used—safety razor, electric shaver—he still looked as though he had run a belt sander across his face. He had inherited his father's thick beard and his mother's sensitive skin. Ralph Martin treated his chaplains like recruits. He had served in the Marine Corps and wore his silver-grey hair in something just beyond the high and tight buzz cut for which the Marines were famous. He already blew hot and cold when it came to Stephen, although he could never figure out why. Martin had trusted Stephen when the shit had hit the fan with Chaplain Marv Goodman at the women's prison a few years back. Goodman had been busted for running a prostitution ring with the trustees when they were outside the prison. Chaplain Goodman had not been such a good man, Travis thought as he smiled wryly.

"Penny for those thoughts of yours," came a voice from behind Stephen.

"That's about all they're worth," Stephen said as he turned, set his tea down and kissed Emily good morning. She was wearing one of his Oxford shirts, with the sleeves rolled up and the buttons not quite done up. He always loved her wearing his shirts as a nightgown. Stephen pushed his face into her cascading wavy brown hair and inhaled. "Gosh I love your scent."

Emily's lips found their way to his and they held a lingering kiss. Stephen moved in close and embraced her. When he started to unbutton her shirt, she playfully pushed him back and said, "Whoa, sailor, I thought your ship sailed to the prison this morning. And I haven't had a cup of tea or coffee yet—unlike some people." She kissed his nose and then gingerly bit his lower lip.

"But the thought of prison makes me horny," Stephen protested.

"You're crazy!" grinned Emily. "Pour me some tea!"

"Crazy for you!" Stephen uttered a low growl and spun around, lifting the cozy off the tea pot. "Madam's tea is ready," he teased, as he fetched a mug from the cupboard. "But we're short on crumpets. How about eggs and toast?"

"Sounds good. If I like them, you might even get lucky...again." Emily smiled over the rim of her mug.

Emily and Stephen engaged in a sort of slow, complicated dance in order to maneuver their way around the tiny kitchen as he began breakfast preparations.

"Let me get out of your way," said Emily as she opened the back door leading onto the little screened porch. The porch was just big enough to hold the hatchway leading down into the basement the oil furnace was located. The cottage sat on the grounds of a larger house. The small patch of grass in the rear led to some woods which bordered a small park. It was located in an older section of Raleigh. Stephen had felt lucky to find this cottage with its single bedroom, small dressing room and bathroom, L-shaped living/dining area and kitchen. It had solid oak floors which bespoke of the 1920s, when it was built. The previous place he had rented was sold from under him and he had needed to move quickly. Happily, a friend with whom he played tennis was in the process of moving from the cottage and put in a good word for him with the owners, who lived in a large house, which sat to the front and off to one side of the cottage. Stephen loved it. In this nicely wooded area of the state capital, he felt a release from the prison units in which he worked. The woods gave a feeling of paradisiacal seclusion.

With the eggs and toast ready, Stephen went onto the porch and lifted the hem of the shirt, patting Emily's firm bottom. "Breakfast is served."

She quickly turned, placed a hand on her hip and waved a finger at him while she said mockingly, "Rev. Travis, you are one horny minister!"

"I think you discovered that when you met me. You invited me over for 'tea and all the fixings,' remember?"

"I seem to recall." She winked at him.

~ * ~

The two had met one Sunday afternoon in June when they both happened to be riding bikes. They had ridden for an hour so before Stephen had to return home. He had said, with flat affect, "This has been great, but I have to go back to prison tonight."

Emily had been lost for words, unsure of whether or not this was a joke. "P-prison?" was all she could stammer.

"Yeah. I work there. I'm a chaplain." Stephen watched for the reaction. Telling other twenty-somethings that he was a minister could often turn out to be a joy-killer.

Emily had considered what she had heard for a moment and then said, "That's cool. My parents are Methodists—well, my mom; my father died when I was very young. So I grew up in the church...but I've kinda drifted away. I suppose I'm more of an agnostic now. I have focused mainly on science since my undergraduate days."

"That's cool too," offered Stephen. "I've never felt faith should be pressed on anyone. Look...I've had a really great time and would like to see you again. Would you mind if I called you sometime?"

"That would be nice. Have you got a piece of paper?"

Stephen looked around helplessly and then shrugged. "Never mind," quipped Emily. "Give me your hand." He proffered his left hand. Emily took it in hers and began to write with a pen she had taken from her saddle bag. Though only momentary, Stephen found the warm touch of her hand scintillating. When she finished writing, she said, "There! Don't sweat it off." She winked and they parted. He looked at his hand and read, "Tea and all the fixings'" followed by an address. Lastly it read, "Wednesday, 4 p.m."

~ * ~

For Stephen, Wednesday couldn't arrive fast enough. Emily Webster lived near NC State University, where she was doing her doctoral research. It was not a long bike ride away, so he decided to pedal over. Emily shared an old, two-story weatherboard house with two other grad students from the university. Stephen pulled his bike up to the porch and leaned it against the railings. The door to the house was open and Travis could see Emily through the screened door. "Knock-knock," he called out.

10

"Come on in!" she called out from the living room. "You're right on time."

"On time was considered five minutes late in my family," Stephen joked as he pulled off his cycling shoes. "My dad is a pilot."

"Poor you," grinned Emily. Patting the sofa where she was sitting, she said, "Have a seat!" On the coffee table sat an area of small cakes, scones, butter and jams.

"It's really good to see you again. I enjoyed our ride last Sunday."

"So how was prison?" Emily asked with her cheeky smile.

"Well, prison is prison. At least I wasn't at the women's prison for the family visitation. I only do that every other week. This past Sunday I led an evening service for the women and then went down the hill to the men's Advancement Center."

Emily munched a scone thoughtfully and then asked, "Advancement Center?"

"Ah, yes," Stephen uttered, his mouth full of cake. "It's an open prison for guys who have spent many years behind bars. It provides them with an adjustment time. They have to work off the premises, pay their room and board—and here's the clincher: they have to find a place to live. That's the hardest bit."

"How come?"

"Because not many people want a former felon living next door to them. Lincoln—he's the social worker with whom I share an office—has to go out and knock on the doors of people living near the house or apartment he and the inmate have agreed on, and then see if folks mind. And they usually mind—except in the worst neighborhoods where most people either have been to prison or have someone close to them serving time. Sadly, it often puts the former inmate back in harm's way—drugs, guns, drinking, gambling and the like."

"So why were you happy to miss family visitation at the women's prison?"

Stephen took a deep breath, letting it out slowly. "Have you ever been to prison visitation—especially with mothers whose children come to see them?"

"I have." Emily looked at him enigmatically and said, "Go on." She sipped her tea.

"All right, we're gonna come back to that one in a minute. But in short, Sundays at the women's prison is a vale of tears. The women sit in chairs facing their loved one or children. They aren't supposed to touch, because that's when drugs and other contraband are transferred. But just try to keep these women from the kids! And when visitation time is up, there is a lot of screaming, crying and wailing—from the mothers and the children. The guards often have to physically separate them. It isn't pretty. I end up having to help police it and it's something that, frankly, I find very difficult. Now, for heaven's sake, can we stop talking about me and prison—with one exception: when did you attend a visiting day?"

Emily studied him for a long while before speaking. "May I ask you one question before answering your question?"

"Certainly."

"Would you consider dating one of the women you work with? I mean after she got out?"

"Well, gosh, I suppose that depends. But if she didn't have a violent past and I liked her..." Stephen's mind pulled up several images of female inmates he had found attractive. "Sure, why not? I guess I could see myself doing that."

"Fair enough," said Emily. "For the record, I haven't attended one visiting day in prison." Stephen looked at her quizzically. "I've attended dozens."

"How so?" Stephen interjected.

12

"I was an inmate." Emily let her words sink with Stephen as she watched him.

"Are you going to tell me more?"

"It depends. Are you still interested?"

"Well, I didn't come for the tea and cakes," Stephen blushed a bit when he realized what he'd just said. "Um, I mean, don't take that the wrong way."

"I think I'll take it as a compliment." She smiled. "Okay then. I spent sixteen months in a Mexican prison. A few college friends and I were spending the summer in Tucson, Arizona. We crossed over into Mexico to buy some pot and got busted."

"Damn! Talk about rough justice. How'd you get such a long sentence on a first offense? I...um...I mean I'm assuming it was a first offense? Oh shit, I'm sorry." Now Stephen really blushed. He couldn't believe how badly things were going.

Emily laughed at his predicament, saying, "Such salty language for a minister. Whatever next? Sex? Relax, okay? This was all nearly nine years ago. I've processed it all, so it almost feels like another life. I got the sentence because it was a warning to other young Americans to stay away. And I didn't have a lawyer. My girlfriend got out some months before me because her parents had the money to buy off the local magistrate or somebody. But my mom was on her own—I think I told you that my dad died when I was tiny—so I had to wait it out. At least some of my friends came to see me. And that is how I know about visitation days."

The two ate in silence for a minute or two. Each time they caught one another's eye, they smiled to the point of choking back laughter. Each wondering what the other found so funny. Stephen noticed that his heart was racing. He found himself ever more attracted to Emily.

Emily was now cross-legged on the sofa facing him. "On the bike ride you mentioned you're doing a doctorate in animal science," he remarked. "What does that involve?"

"Animals," She quipped.

"You're clever, aren't you?" Stephen leaned over and tried to stuff a jam-covered scone into her mouth. Emily quickly grabbed his thumb at the wrist and twisted it, although he had managed to smear the jam over her mouth and chin.

She held his thumb in her surprisingly strong grip; to the point that Stephen winced. She pointed her free index finger at him with dead seriousness in her eyes, and then pointed at her chin. "You know you're going to have to clean this off, don't you?" With that she pulled him toward her until they were face-to-face. "Start cleaning, Chaplain."

What followed was a mêlée of tongues, jam, scone and lips, but mainly tongues and lips. When they came up for air, Emily grinned and said, "You didn't come just for the tea and cake, did you?" She stood up and took him by the hand. "Let's go upstairs." Stephen gladly did as he was instructed. On the way up the stairs, Emily stopped, turned and looked at him. "You know, you wouldn't have survived as a chaplain in my prison."

She continued leading Stephen up the stairs. "Why?" he asked.

"We would have fucked you to death!"

~ * ~

A mockingbird woke Stephen up. He was sprawled across a large, old four-poster bed. His and Emily's clothes were spread across the floor. He looked out the open window and saw the culprit bird on the branch of a magnolia not far from the house. It was merrily singing its head off. Emily was half-turned beside him with her flowing locks covering her face. They lifted gently as she breathed. The intoxicating smell of wisteria drifted in through

14

the window. Stephen lay there for a few minutes, contemplating both the evening and the night before. By his reckoning, he and Emily had gone to bed about 6 p.m. They had spent hours making love, laughing, talking and then making love again until they fell asleep. Stephen mused how much more satisfying sleep was after making love.

He noticed that the bedside clock showed 6:30. He silently cursed the winged siren who had awakened him from such a deep and pleasant sleep. Stephen's bladder was also waking up, so he decided to chance a dash to the bathroom as the house seemed quiet enough. He hadn't heard either housemate come home. Trying not to disturb Emily, he slipped from the sheets and tiptoed from the bedroom, opening the door as softly as possible. There were several doors along the landing from which to choose. The wooden floorboard creaked a bit as he crept along. He was feeling a bit silly, as he was nude. Finally, he saw a partially opened door and peeped inside. Bingo! Stephen walked across the cool tile floor, relieved himself and then went to the handbasin to wash his hands and face. He could smell Emily's scent on his fingers. His dark hair was in a style that only sleep and damp bodies can devise. He looked at himself in the mirror and noticed that his smile was that of the satiated. Peering out the bathroom door to make sure the coast was clear, Stephen headed back to Emily's room. He was shocked, however, to see someone standing just to the side of door with a towel over his shoulder.

"Well, hello sailor!" chirped the young man standing before him, looking Stephen up and down with appreciation. "Someone's been a very lucky and very naughty girl." He let out a theatrical sigh, "Oh, that I should be so lucky. Bye, sweetheart." The speaker laughed gayly as he closed the bathroom door.

Abashed, Stephen made tracks for Emily's bedroom. She was stirring as he climbed back into the four-poster. "I see you've met Charles...you've probably made his day—or week." She yawned. "He hasn't had much luck with love—or lust—since he moved here." Emily shook the hair from her face and pulled him in close to her. "I'm glad he didn't ravage you!"

Within minutes of her waking, Emily was sitting astride him, brushing her hair across his face as they made love. "Hope you weren't in a hurry to get back to prison," she purred at him.

"What prison?" replied Stephen as he pulled her face toward his.

~ * ~

Their hunger for one another sated for the moment, Emily treated them to a breakfast consisting of leftover scones and cakes, but a fresh pot of tea. While they ate and smiled at one another sheepishly, Charles walked through the kitchen and opened the back door. "Your friend has a nice ass!" was all he said as he swished out the screen door, laughing as it slammed shut.

Stephen felt his face turn red as he asked Emily, "Um...what's his story?"

"Oh, Charles. Our young Mr. Hampton is as gay as they come. Or as he likes to put it when he's in the mood to shock, 'I'm as queer as a three-dollar bill!'"

"You mimicked his voice well," chuckled Stephen. "He seems good humored about it all."

"Oh, he is. He's a good roomie. Always pays his share of the rent on time. He's actually very kind. I suppose I should have warned you, but then it's kinda fun that I didn't." Emily tossed her head back and let go a belly laugh. "Gosh, I wish I could have seen your reaction."

"You saw enough!" Stephen filled his mouth with scone and licked jam from his fingers. "Despite this being a university town, doesn't Charles find it hard to feel free—to be who he is?"

"To hear him tell it, no; but I think it is rather difficult for him. But then, he comes from a small town in South Carolina, so Raleigh is positively metropolitan. He's a whiz in cell biology—and well respected by the staff. He seems secure enough to make his own way."

A brief silence ensued as they sipped tea and munched breakfast. Before long Stephen cleared his throat and said, "I have a question for you."

Emily simply raised her eyebrows in unspoken language indicating, "Okay."

"What did you mean last night when, uh, when you said that if I had been a chaplain in your prison I would have been fucked to death?"

Emily let out a brief snort of laughter as she said, "So you were listening—and not just looking at my ass as we went upstairs." She paused, took a deep breath and asked, "Are you sure you want to hear this?"

"How will I know until I hear it?" Stephen shrugged.

"What do women do in the prison where you work—for sex, I mean?"

Stephen gulped down the last of his tea, rubbed his unshaved chin and chuckled to himself as he remembered how his predecessor at the women's prison had been caught in the kitchen freezer *in flagrante delicto* with one of the inmates. Stephen briefly shared the story with Emily, who howled with laughter at the idea of the chaplain being caught with his trousers down and in the act.

"So," Stephen continued, "That's how some women take care of their needs. Others form partnerships with other women, and the rest..." He lifted his arms in the universal sign for 'who knows?'

"Masturbation isn't an infraction. But, in fact, not many of the women mention sex when they come to see me."

"What's the average sentence for inmates there? And how many women?"

"Oh, I guess it's about twelve years; and there are just over six hundred women." Stephen replied.

"So, are you telling me, Stephen Travis, that with all of those caged up women, they haven't tried to hit on you?!"

"Well, some have...of course; but mostly they give me cat calls, whistles and make...um, rather explicit statements when I walk across the yard between the buildings. One or two tried to offer themselves to me—but that isn't gonna happen!" Stephen found himself blushing again and feeling almost like a schoolboy. "Why do you ask?"

"Oh, it's just that a good-looking, twen—how old are you anyway?"

"Twenty-nine," Stephen blurted, "And what has that to do with your prison, which you have deftly avoided?"

"Oh, I wasn't avoiding, I was just wondering...and kinda picturing you—as you are—in 'my prison.'" Emily shook her head at the image it produced.

"Okay, out with it! What's going on in that beautiful head of yours?"

"Beautiful, huh? Mmh, I like that." Emily let out a loud puff of breath. "We had a prison garden—where a number of us worked and grew food for ourselves. There was a local woman who oversaw all of us and taught us how to plant the seeds, how deep to place them, how much water they needed, etc. She had this young son—he couldn't have been more than seventeen—and some of us would keep *mamacita* busy with questions, while others would take Manuel into the tool shed and...well, you can picture the rest."

"Cradle robber!" Stephen said with a straight face. Emily kept her eyes on him to see whether or not he was actually outraged. He smiled, shook his head and—speaking as much to

18

himself as to Emily—said, "I guess it was a case of needs must. I've never been locked up before—well, except for hitchhiking in the state of Virginia when I was a college student; but that was only a few days, so it hardly counts. What can I say?"

"Still want to see me?"

"Yes," he responded immediately. Emily smiled at him across the table.

"But only if you're not chasing seventeen-year-olds anymore!" With a flick of her hand, Emily landed a piece of buttered scone, sticky with jam, on Stephen's forehead. He sat with crossed eyes looking upwards, as the scone slowly slid and then dropped onto his plate. They burst out laughing.

"I hate to end all of this fun and frivolity, but I have to go to work. But first I have to cycle home." Emily feigned a pouty face. "Oh, may I ask you one more question before I leave?"

Emily nodded, "Sure."

"What is your last name?"

~ * ~

Now it was September, and over the intervening three months since they had met, Stephen and Emily Webster had found themselves increasingly spending more of their free time together. Emily came in from the miniature back porch and sat down at the table with him. She leaned over and smelled the scrambled eggs. She stuck her fork in and filled her mouth.

Depending upon one's view on table manners, Emily had the habit of speaking with her mouth full. She seemed to enjoy it—as well as the reactions she received. "So," mmph, "Shaplain Stee-fan Twavis," she slurped and swallowed, chasing the eggs with tea. "You seem a little preoccupied this morning. Want to tell this animal scientist all about it?"

"There's really not a lot to say...but it's all very strange." Stephen slowly drew his right index finger across his top lip—something Emily noticed he did when concentrating. "Just about everybody at the advancement center thought he heard two gunshots last night—early evening really. And one of our guys absconded. I can't figure it out. Both things might be totally unrelated."

"We-e-ell," drawled Emily, "In the lab we'd run the experiment again.

Stephen rolled his eyes and made a little growl.

"No, really, I mean what's somebody doing with a gun at the advancement center? You've taught me enough to know that it's an open prison, for God's sake."

"Yeah, there's that and then there's why did Walter Jackson up and run? Nobody had a clue as to why he'd do that. It's just weird."

"What will happen when—or if—they catch him?"

"Oh, they'll catch him, all right. They always do. Most people head for home or at least somewhere in their old neighborhood. Unless he has a damned good excuse, they can send him back to serve out the rest of his sentence. Poor guy. He seemed to be doing so well. That's what's so crazy about it all."

"It's funny, all of this..." mused Emily.

"How so?"

"I don't mean what happened in the prison yesterday—I mean us. It's funny in an interesting sort of way. The fact that I've fallen for a prison chaplain—or for a minister at all! Don't get me wrong—I like it—"

"Well, I should hope so!" Stephen chimed in with a wink.

"I mean...well, did you ever think you'd be having breakfast—on a regular basis—with an animal scientist who hangs out in barns and laboratories, studies different types of digestive systems and metabolisms and the like?"

"Frankly, no. But I like it. I also like the way you explore this particular human animal!" Stephen winked again at Emily.

"Whoa, big fella! Down!" Emily extended her hand, palm forward. "We both have to be outta here soon."

"And tonight? Whose house?"

"Let's make it mine. I'll try to keep Charles off you!"

Three

Stephen pulled his aging Pontiac LeMans into the parking lot of the advancement center. September was feeling almost as hot as August had been. He was glad there was a modicum of air-conditioning in this unit—compared to the women's prison up the hill and most other prisons. Mike Watson was on the main desk, as Stephen stepped inside. "Hey, Chaplain. Looks like another hot one, eh?"

Stephen poked his head around the doors to the other staff offices and greeted everyone. Maxine Willerby was the secretary. She had a nasally, high-pitched Southern accent. "Well, hey there, Stephen! How are yew?" Maxine had hair like the cotton candy he had eaten at the fair when he was a child. Her pale, white skin almost seemed to vanish given her choice of light pink lipstick. Stephen kept having the vision of Maxine slowly disappearing, leaving behind only her nasally voice, her hair and eyeglasses on the chain around her neck. "Kin I dew anything for yew tew-day, Stephen?"

"Nah, thanks, Maxine. Just wanted to say good morning. Oh, is Warden Harris in?"

"Ya-yus," Maxine nodded vigorously. "Yew kin go right in." Maxine's head was still nodding like a mechanical doll.

Warden Samson Harris was sitting at his desk, looking lost. He always looked lost. It was as though he woke up in someone else's life, suddenly finding himself the warden of a pre-release facility in the North Carolina Department of Corrections. He must have had some political connections because no one became a warden without someone pushing him or her forward. Even his name 'Samson' was a misnomer, given his diminutive stature and his tendency always to appear frightened. Perhaps that is why he had the good sense to go by 'Sam?' Sam's dark skin accentuated the whites of his eyes, giving him that 'deer caught in the headlights' appearance. However it was that Sam came to be the warden of this particular open prison, he rarely, if ever, acted like the man in charge. Travis had been in the corrections business long enough to have known quite a few wardens—male and female—so Harris was an odd one.

"Good morning, Warden Harris. Mind if I come in?"

Looking up with near alarm in his countenance, Harris tumbled out his response, "No, no, um...come on in, Chaplain." Harris indicated a chair.

"Warden Harris, can you shed any light on what happened last night? I was on duty here with Fowler and Strader. We heard two gunshots—or at least Fowler and I did, not to mention most of the residents. Fowler and I looked around but couldn't see anyone or find anything. And then, after a bunk check, Jackson turned out to be missing."

Harris's eyes were shifting back and forth like a ventriloquist's dummy. He nervously played with a pen. "No, nope, nothing I can add." Harris raised his hands as though saying, "I didn't do it!"

"What do you think will happen with Jackson—once he's found?"

Without hesitation, but far worse in Stephen's opinion— almost without thought—Harris said, "Oh, he'll be sent back to finish his sentence."

Travis felt himself bristle at Harris' words. Stephen often found himself being an advocate for the men in the advancement center. People with no experience of corrections wrongly saw the center as 'easy time' or 'coddling the inmates.' They had no idea that for men who had spent fifteen, twenty or more years behind bars, the months or weeks leading up to release were actually among the most stressful since their first entry into prison. The world outside had simply changed too much and was beyond their recognition. They might as well have been turned loose in Namibia with a map of North Carolina. Their former knowledge was of very little use. And to make matters even worse, most people they had known had either died or forgotten them.

"But, Warden Harris, we don't even know why Jackson ran—or even *if* he ran. Shouldn't he be given the benefit of the doubt?"

At that moment, Harris, began looking preoccupied with finding something on his desk. In Travis' opinion it was a pretense so he didn't have to look directly at Travis. "Well, well...um, we'll see when we find him, you never know, you never know. I, uh, have something I need to do now." That was the chaplain's cue to leave.

Stephen spun around and walked to his office. *Yeah*, he thought, *you have something to do all right—ignore the problem that's right under your nose.*

Travis, in his inner fury, swung open the door to his shared office without expecting to see Parker. "Yo, Rev! What's with the dramatic entry, man?"

"Oh, sorry Linc!" Stephen looked and pointed back toward the front offices. "I've been with Harris." Stephen shook his head in frustration.

"And how is our resident Uncle Tom?" Lincoln leaned back in his chair and smiled at Stephen. Two things Stephen had come to know about Lincoln Parker. First, he didn't tend to get stressed over things. Second, he was the best-dressed social worker Travis had ever known. The man was always immaculate—even in the midst of wilting summer heat, his collars were neat and never flopping from perspiration like with Travis or other ordinary human beings. Lincoln epitomized 'cool' in every sense of the word. Many of the residents referred to him as "GQ"—short for the men's fashion magazine, *Gentlemen's Quarterly*. Although a few years younger than Travis, he knew his way around the prison system and state law, and thereby gave the residents at the advancement center solid advice.

Travis dropped into his chair at the desk facing Parker's. "Well, Harris is Harris."

"Yeah," grinned Lincoln. He tapped the eraser of his pencil on the desk, accentuating each word. "That man lives in somebody's hip pocket. You can count on it."

"Has he ever made a decision since he's been here?" Stephen had only come to the center on a regular basis in the last year, and that was two to three days a week.

"I don't know that Harris has ever made a decision!" replied Lincoln. "Frankly, apart from his wife, I don't know how he even dresses himself in the morning. And speaking of the lovely Mrs. Harris—have you ever met the woman?"

"Can't say I have. Why?"

At this point Lincoln switched from his native Maryland and UNC graduate school voice to Raleigh street talk. "Dat woman big! Damn big!" He drew her shape in the air, as Stephen chuckled. Once Parker had Travis laughing, he liked to keep it going. "Shee-ut, man, Harris' woman tower over him, man, she snap 'im half do she wan' to, unh-hunh." Travis was belly laughing now. "I don't be jivin' 'bout dis, white boy. No way! You hear me talkin'?"

"Yes—and enough! They're gonna think we've gone mad in here," Stephen nodded at the door.

"Why, whatever for?" Lincoln had changed gears with the blink of an eye. "Good heavens, Reverend, get a grip on yourself."

Wiping the tears of laughter from his eyes, Stephen asked, "Linc, are you aware of what went down here last night?"

"I suppose so, two gunshots and Jackson took off. That about the size of it? Oh, and about a quarter of the residents act like nothing happened."

Stephen nodded and then added, "And it's only made worse because Harris—" and here Stephen lowered his voice—"is happy to throw the book at Jackson whenever he turns up. We don't even know why he ran or even if he ran. I mean what if he were shot and then carried off—by someone on the outside? There are any number of possibilities."

"Ah, but even one possibility is too many for our good warden," offered Parker. "Look, man, don't get yourself too worked up about this. You know prison. It's a different world and it has its own rules. Just take it easy. More information is bound to come. Just give it time."

At that moment someone knocked at the door. Stephen jumped up and opened it. Delbert Moore was standing outside the office, with one hand resting on the wall. "Hey, Chaplain Travis, may I have a word?" With a nod to Parker, who had obviously been working when Travis arrived, Stephen offered that they go to the exercise yard. There were benches where he and Delbert could sit.

Delbert was clearly the best educated man in the unit— apart from Stephen, which is why he liked to talk with him. It was rarely, if ever, that he spoke about things spiritual or faith, but rather more about keeping his spirits up while serving out his sentence. The fact was, Moore was working on his master's degree in Elizabethan literature by extension from the University of North Carolina. More often than not, Delbert liked Stephen to read his work before he submitted it—something Stephen enjoyed doing. Delbert had been working with his local town council—of which he was a member—to have the sheriff, Elton Stokes, removed from office for corruption. Before they could spring the net, some sheriff's deputies raided Delbert's house where they conveniently found half a dozen marijuana plants growing in his back yard. The fact that Delbert was never known to have smoked dope and the fact that the soil around the root balls of the plants was different from the soil in Delbert's back yard carried no weight as evidence in court, so Delbert found himself being jailed. The sheriff sat in the front row of the court, smiling all the while, as the jury found Delbert guilty. He had known the outcome before he set foot in the courthouse. The only saving grace was that Delbert—as a first-time 'offender'—was sent to the Fairborn Advancement Center for Men, instead of being locked up 24/7. Delbert was not in the pre-release program, as he had not served 'hard time,' so apart from occasional trips to the library, he carried out his studies in the center. The solitude made his eighteen months seem like ten years.

Once Travis and Moore were seated, Travis enquired, "What's on your mind today?"

"It's a shitty day in the neighborhood, a crapacious day for a neighbor. Does that give you a clue?"

Travis chuckled at the imaginative response. "Yeah, I get it."

"Oh, it's the same old shit, Chaplain. I'm obsessed with the fact that we were so close to exposing the goddamned sheriff. There had to have been an informant on the council! And that bastard Stokes is still going about business as usual. Hell, he knows who's growing pot because the big growers give him protection money. Same with illegal booze, and God knows what else. It's so fucking unfair! The worst thing is that I don't know who to trust anymore. Whenever I get a visitor, I can't help but think 'Is it you who sold me out to Stokes?' It's eating me up inside."

"All the more reason for you to keep your head in your studies. God knows I'd be pissed off if I were in your shoes, but if you focus on this shit, it will destroy you."

"I know. I know...it's just that I...well sometimes I just have to get it out. I know you've heard it all before." Delbert shook his head and looked at his feet. He was a picture of despair.

"Look, man, it's why I'm here," Stephen said. "Sometimes I think of myself as an antacid tablet." Delbert's head came up. "And other times, well...I think of myself as toilet paper." Now Moore chuckled. "I feel I am here to absorb some of the shit that has been dumped on people. But I get to go home and do my best to leave as much as I can along the way."

Delbert nodded slowly. "Guess I hadn't thought of your role in that way. I almost feel sorry for you!"

"Well don't. I am doing this out of free choice—and I truly believe this is what God has asked me to do."

"No shit?"

"No shit. I had planned to be an academic. I was going to get my PhD in Hebrew Bible and hopefully get a job at some college or university. But God had other plans for me. I had never given prison chaplaincy a thought...but then, as I came into my second year of seminary, I was asked to visit someone from a church I attended who was in the women's prison—right up there." Stephen pointed at the fence up the hill. "And the rest, as they say, is history."

"It certainly isn't a university setting, is it?"

"Well, Delbert, university or prison, I think one institution is as good as another in God's eyes. And besides, prison is certainly an education! Right? I mean, you're not going to sit there and tell me you haven't learned anything since you've been here, are you?"

Delbert nodded slowly, "I guess I can't disagree. I have learned one thing: that I don't want to spend another minute more here than I have to—that's for sure!"

"And most of the guys here have spent the majority of your lifetime locked up."

"Message received, Chaplain. Blessed are the inmates, for theirs is the true understanding of freedom—eh?"

"I don't think Mr. Jesus would disagree with that!"

"Think I'll get back to my books. Thanks, Rev." Delbert got up, stretched, and strolled back into the building.

Before Stephen could move, he heard someone addressing him. "Yeah, Rev, you got a minute?" It was Tyrone Mason, one of the inmates who, when he wasn't out working, was in the exercise yard working out—lifting weights and training. He had the build of a middle-weight boxer—such a physique came in handy when doing hard time. He kept his head shaved, making it look like polished ebony, and wore a neat goatee.

As Tyrone approached him, Stephen mused about how many inmates preferred to meet a chaplain outside of an office or chapel. At the women's prison, he used to hang out by the basketball court. Sooner or later someone would seemingly need a rest and perch on the bench near the chaplain. *But, hey,*" he thought, *whatever works.*

"You doin' all right, Rev?"

"Sure am, Tyrone. What about you?" They shook hands, using the 'brothers' handshake,' although in this prison it had four parts to it: 'normal' palm-to-palm handshake, switching to the thumb grasp, followed by a finger clasp topped off by a double fist tap on top of the clasped fingers. For a white guy, Travis had caught on fairly quickly.

"I'm fine, I'm fine. Be even better once I be outta this place, but then...it's better than the joint."

"That's for sure." Over the last five years, Stephen had worked in about seven different units—the worst being Raleigh's Central Prison. The advancement center was a holiday camp by comparison.

"Listen, man, what you make of the other night?" Mason kept a steady gaze on Travis.

Stephen knew what Tyrone was referencing. "I don't know, man. It was—and is—weird. And truth to tell—" and at this point he looked back at the building to make sure no one could hear him—"I couldn't get anything useful from Warden Harris."

Tyrone's beautiful smile broke like sunshine on his face. He shook his head as though in pity and asked Stephen, "Now, Rev, what you go ask that useless Tom for? You been here long enough to know better." With his long index finger, he poked firmly on Travis' chest with each word. "Rev, you—know—that—Harris—don't—run—this—place." Tyrone left his finger in Travis' pectoral muscle to let his words sink in. "But do you know who actually run it?" As lightly as a cat, Tyrone sprang to his feet.

"I can't really say that I do," Stephen responded, as he got to his feet.

Already walking away, Mason stopped, made a half turn, and said, "Rev, Jackson was doing fine. He didn't have no reason to run." Tyrone's eyes held Stephen's gaze. Then he smiled again and said, "Rev, you need to work out!" With that he slapped his muscled chest hard and walked off, laughing at the top of his voice.

Four

Stephen pulled up outside Emily's house, looked up at the sash window of her room and felt warm and comfortable inside. At twenty-nine, he had done his share of dating over the years. Yet something was starting to feel different this time. They had spent nearly every night together since their first night. He liked that she had her own field of interest—and that it was so very different from his. Stephen got out of his car, stretched, and then did a ritual shaking off the dust of prison. He had tried to make a point of not letting the trials and tribulations of inmates in various prisons spill over into his home life. He mounted the stairs to the front porch and opened the door. He dropped his keys onto the side and table, and then looked down the hallway into the kitchen, where Emily and Charles were preparing dinner. As he entered the kitchen, Emily wiped her hands on her apron and gave him a big hug and kiss.

"There's my favorite jailbird," she quipped.

"And my favorite ex-con," he replied.

"What about me, sweet cheeks?" pouted Charles. "You two gonna stand there and torture me?"

"Trust me, Charlie baby, if being gay did it for me, you'd be the first...well, maybe not one of the first to know, but..." Charles threw a hand towel at Stephen. "What's for dinner tonight?"

"Spaghetti Caroliner," Charles waved his spatula indicatively, "with pajamarama chayse." Charles exaggerated his South Carolina accent. "Y'all hon-gree?"

"We certainly are," Emily answered for Stephen. "Where's our other roomie, Charles?"

"Said she was going up for a soak in the bath. She knows to get herself down here or suffer the consequences. Between us mad scientists and the ravenous prison chaplain, locusts couldn't do a better job!"

The other housemate was Patricia Crawford. She too was a graduate student at NC State. She hailed from the tiny mill town of Saxapahaw, North Carolina. Her father had been the chief engineer for the cotton mill there and his life-long interest in electrical engineering had rubbed off on his daughter. Apart from breakfast and dinner Pat's only interest in the house was a place to sleep. She had a head full of tight blonde curls and wore thick glasses—the sort which look like the bottoms of soda bottles. She had owl-like movements which were accentuated whenever she was asked a question. She would slowly turn her head in the direction of the person who asked the question. Having located the person, she would blink once or twice, squint—as though focusing in on the interlocutor (which she might well have been doing)—and then adjust her glasses before answering. Stephen kept waiting for her to respond with 'Whooo?'

As Emily dished out the salad and Charles scooped out the spaghetti, Pat came and sat at the table. She smelled of over-perfumed soap. Pat looked from one to the other of the three seated at the table, blinking as her gaze fixed upon each—as though taking a mental photo. "I'm famished," was all she said and then her hands and mouth were in constant motion. Charles, Emily and Stephen all traded surreptitious grins as they watched—and heard—her eat. Pat finished long before the others, wiped her mouth on her napkin; and, compared to her style of eating, belched daintily into the napkin. She then gave her table-mates her goggle blink, said, "That was good," and left the table.

The three moderately paced diners did their best not to meet one another's gaze for fear of laughing. They had no desire to hurt Pat's feelings. Charles whispered to Stephen, "See all of the spices and condiments on the counter-top?" Stephen looked and nodded. "What do you notice about them?"

"Well," mused Travis, "They are all arranged in ascending—or descending—order."

"Precisely!" beamed Charles. "Your lady love and I have noticed over the months that Pat's been with us, that—whenever she gets stressed—everything in the house starts getting placed in such order—even our books!"

"Does that bother you?" queried Stephen.

"At first, it did," added in Emily. "But then we saw how it helped Pat cope—but more than that, she goes on a cleaning frenzy throughout the house, which neither of us minds!"

Stephen did the washing up as he had been the recipient of a nicely prepared meal. Emily did the drying and Charles hit the books. "You three are certainly an interesting bunch."

"Yes, well I'm the normal one," chirped Emily. "That is...if testing animal dung and urine is 'normal'."

"You're normal as I need you to be," responded Stephen, as he leaned over and kissed her neck just below the ear.

"Mmh, I like that." She smiled, but as he pulled away from Emily's neck, her head suddenly tilted to one side. "Quick," she said, grabbing him by the arm, "Your kiss has left me imbalanced! I need you to do it on the other side."

Needing no further encouragement, Stephen moved to Emily's right side and began to kiss her neck. When he came up for air, her head dropped backwards and she urgently pointed to her neck below the Adam's Apple. Uttering a low moan, Emily whispered, "Have you finished the dish washing?"

Stephen gave Emily a gentle love smack on her bottom. "You leetle minx," he intoned, with the best French accent he could muster, as he continued kissing her neck.

"Here's the critical question."

"What's that?" asked the preoccupied Stephen.

"Are you on duty tonight?" As Stephen shook his head in the negative, he quickly went into a crouch, grabbed Emily behind her thighs, took her left arm in his, scooped her up into a 'fireman's carry' and headed for the stairs. "Um," asked Emily, "Can I leave this tea towel in the kitchen?"

"Fling it," came his response.

Once on the landing, Stephen pushed the bedroom door open with his foot, crossed the room, and gently plopped Emily on the bed.

Flushed from her ride up the stairs, Emily took in a large breath and, exhaling, said, "Rev. Travis, I never thought of you as the caveman type!"

"Well, one of the inmates told me today that I needed to work out. Soooo..." And with that he hopped onto the bed, straddled Emily on his hands and knees and began kissing her face, nose, cheeks and neck.

Catching him off-guard, Emily tickled his ribs. As he pulled back, she flipped him onto his back, and pulled off her cotton blouse, saying, "I'll give you a workout!"

Five

Stephen arose early, leaving a drowsy Emily in her disheveled bed. He dressed quickly and went out to the car. The air had the first hint of autumn. He had an involuntary shudder—was it the cool air or was it the fact that he was going straight to the head office for North Carolina Corrections with the hope of catching Ralph Martin, the director of chaplaincy services, in his office? The decade-old LeMans complained a bit when he turned the ignition but finally started and he drove the few miles into central Raleigh.

Stephen went to Martin's office with some trepidation. In the years he had worked under Ralph's leadership, Stephen had often been treated with warmth and appreciation. Other times, Ralph acted as though Stephen were an annoyance. After Stephen had held the fort at the women's prison following the dismissal and arrest of his former chaplain supervisor—while finishing his last year of seminary—Martin had asked Stephen to take on the advancement center, as well as do some work at the youth center. That had seemed like a vote of confidence in Stephen's abilities as a chaplain. But when there had been a special service to honor the correctional system's chaplains, and to which all wardens and chaplains were invited, Ralph had completely skipped over Stephen, the advancement center, and Warden Harris—much to their mutual embarrassment and puzzlement. Now, nearly a year after that snub, Stephen could think of no particular reason why Ralph was so changeable in his attitude.

He entered the drab, grey stone building and went upstairs to Ralph's office. The blue haze of cigarette smoke hung in the air outside Martin's office. Peggy—Martin's secretary—seemed immune both to the smoke and Martin's unpredictable mood.

"Hey, there, Chaplain Stephen! You're here early!" Peggy was like a human bubble bath. She had so many bubbles that Ralph's darker moods couldn't burst them all. She always addressed the chaplains by their first names—following that Southern tradition of calling the minister 'Pastor-So-and-so.'

"Hey, Peggy. Is Ralph in? I'd like to see him for a few minutes."

"He's in, but let me check." Stephen thought he saw her raise her eyebrows at him. Was she acknowledging Martin's fast-changing mood-seasons? Rather than call him, she left her desk and tapped on his door while opening it. "Ralph? Stephen Travis's here to see you. Have you got a few minutes?"

"Yeah, send him on in." Peggy smiled over her should at Stephen. "He's all yours."

Ralph was lighting another cigarette as Stephen entered. He squinted through the smoke and said, "What can I do you for, Stephen?" With his cigarette hand, he waved at a chair. Ralph leaned back in his chair and crossed his legs on the edge of the desk.

"Good morning, Ralph, and thanks for seeing me without an appointment. Have you heard anything from the advancement center in the last few days?"

Ralph took a long drag on his cigarette and blew it out slowly while shaking his head. "Not a thing. Why?"

"You didn't hear anything about gunfire on the grounds there a couple of nights ago? And one of the inmates disappearing?"

Martin slowly lowered his feet. Like an actor, he seemed to need exaggerated movements when he was about to make a point. "Stephen, you know damn well we have a chain of command. Oughtn't you to be talking with Warden Harris about this?"

"I have spoken with him. He doesn't seem concerned. But the man who disappeared, Walter Jackson, was so near release. He had a job, and Parker—the social worker—had a near cert' on a home plan. I can't help but think the gunfire and Jackson's disappearance are related. I simply wanted to register my concern with you."

Martin stubbed out his cigarette. "Yeah, well now you've done so. Just leave it to the prison professionals, Stephen. Is there anything else?" Martin indicated the paperwork on his desk.

Stephen felt his cheeks burning. Martin's flippant "leave it to the prison professionals" had stung—as it was probably meant to do. He shook his head. "Thanks. No. That's it." He turned on his heels and exited Martin's office. He sped past Peggy's desk and gave her a little wave as he went into the hallway. It seemed to dawn on him that a lot of his bike riding was more than pleasure—it was his way burning off the aggravation of working in this goddamned prison service! How was it that gunfire in an open prison and a missing inmate were beyond the remit of the chaplain? Wasn't it part of pastoral concern for the wellbeing of both residents and staff?

Stephen got in his car and began the journey to the advancement center.

Once inside, Stephen was glad to see James Fowler on the main desk. He didn't bother going to greet Maxine or Harris, but walked straight to Fowler and pulled up a chair. "How's it going?" he asked.

"It'll pass muster," smiled James. "How about yourself?"

Stephen held out his hand and wobbled it, "*Comme ci, comme ça.*"

"I remember that much French from Saigon," nodded Fowler. "So what's up?"

"James, have you managed to learn anything else from the other night?"

"Apart from submitting my report to Harris and his accepting it, nothing. You?"

Stephen shook his head as he rubbed his chin, "Nah. And I've just come from Ralph Martin's office." Fowler perked up upon hearing the name of one of the system's 'higher ups.'

"And?"

"And he basically told me to keep things within the 'chain of command' and that it was none of my business anyway. He might as well have told me to concern myself with the souls of the inmates and not their whole wellbeing. It was weird—*he* was weird!"

James was about eight years older than Stephen, and he felt like a sort of older brother he had never had. Fowler smiled warmly at Travis. "Well, don't get too churned up about it. Something is bound to come out—sooner or later."

As Stephen neared his office, he saw Marvin Jacobs waiting outside the door, nervously shifting from foot to foot. He held an envelope in his hand. "Hey, Rev, man it's good to see you. Kinda like to talk with you."

"Yeah Marvin, no problem. Let me get the lights on in here. Come on in."

Marvin took a quick glance down the corridor housing the front offices and then went in. "Mind if I close the door? This here is...well, confidential." He looked straight at Travis. "Very." Marvin handed him the manila envelope. "Have a look at this."

Stephen took the envelope and poured its contents onto his desk. There were some notes with various amounts of money written on them. One had the name of Walter Jackson's wife on it. And then there was a home-made bill of sale for a car which also had Thelma Jackson's name on it. Stephen also saw a scrawled signature which seemed to belong to a Vance Strader. He lifted his eyes at Jacobs, who had been watching him intently. "Where did you get these?"

Marvin dropped his voice to a whisper. "Best you don't know." He looked around the office as though checking for an eavesdropper. "I heard you been axin' for some answers to the other night's little happening. Now, I know we can trust you."

"Are these Jackson's property?" Again, Marvin glanced around and simply nodded. "Are we talking about some financial deal between Jackson and Strader?"

Jacobs just looked at Travis with a poker face, which he finally broke by raising his shoulders and arms in a Gallic shrug, which is universal for 'Who knows?'

Jacobs simply said, "Hang onto those papers. And don't tell nobody you don't trust you got 'em. Understand? I got to talk to some other people. I'll get back to you, okay? Don't come axin' for me. But if you need to see me, you take one of them little two-and-a-half pound weights that hardly nobody uses when pumpin' iron?—and you put it on the corner of that old picnic table outside. Got it?"

"Yeah, I've got it." Although truthfully, Stephen hadn't a clue what he had 'got.' If he indeed had anything, it was more than likely the tail end of a copperhead that could easily twist around and bite him. Whatever it was, it didn't bode well.

"One more thing?" asked Marvin. "Could you just make a tiny peep outside your office to see if any other staff are in sight?"

Stephen discreetly opened the door a bit. Happily, the opening side faced the security staff offices. Pushing it a bit further, he looked the other way. No one was about. Stephen simply looked at Marvin and nodded toward the door, giving him a thumbs up.

Quietly as a baby's breathing, Marvin slipped out the door. Stephen closed the door and went back to his desk to think. First, he shoved the paperwork back into the envelope and put it in his desk drawer. He knew the documents could not remain there. Even the locking file cabinet could be opened with a pen knife. No safety there—but where? Then the answer hit him: Katz! Dr. Benjamin Katz was the clinical psychologist at the women's prison. He and Stephen had become good friends over the years they had worked together. Katz was not only a very good therapist but also had a wicked sense of humor—which was necessary to survive mentally and emotionally when working behind bars for any length of time.

Stephen lifted the receiver and dialed Katz's number, hoping he was in the office and not with an inmate. Before the second ring, he heard a click and then "Katz." Ben was never one to waste words.

"Is this Dial-a-Jewish-joke?"

"It certainly is. So Moishe hasn't been feeling so well and goes to see his GP. His GP says he'll run some tests—blood work and that sort of thing, and that he'd see Moishe in a week. A week goes by and Moishe returns to his doctor and asks, "Nu? What's the news?' The GP says, 'Moishe, I want you to sit down.' Moishe asks, 'What? Is it that bad?' The doc nods and says, 'Is your will up to date?' Moishe collapses into a chair, head in hands, mumbling 'Oy veh!' Then he looks up and asks the doctor, 'How long?' The doctor says, 'Sorry Moishe, three—maybe four months at most.' Moishe starts to weep, 'Veh ist mir!' But then he stops, looks up and asks his doctor, 'Isn't there anything that can be done?' The doctor thinks for a moment and asks Moishe, 'Are you married?' Surprised, Moishe asks, 'No, why?' Then doctor simply says, 'Go out. Find yourself a nice Jewish girl and marry her— ASAP!' Clinging to this bit of hope, Moishe says, 'Fine, Doc, fine. So this will help?' The doctor says, 'No, but four months will seem like forty years!'"

Stephen cracked up. "Ah, Ben, you never fail! Where do you learn all of these jokes?"

"Are you kidding me? They come *in utero*, it's a package deal for God's chosen people. The Torah forbids being a Jew without a sense of humor. It's a serious offense. You on the grounds today?"

"Not yet. I'm down the hill. Listen, could I borrow you for half-an-hour sometime soon? I really need to run something by you."

"Can you make it now?"

"Absolutely!"

"Fine. See you then." Stephen heard the phone click. Katz wasn't one for the usual formalities. He had brought his curt, New Yorker ways to this most Southern of towns and prisons. Travis thought of Ben as something like the character in *A New England Yankee in King Arthur's Court*, except modernized into *A New York Jew in Jesse Helms' State*. Helms was a right-wing senator who was an embarrassment to many of the Republicans who voted for him. He was one of the voices for the big tobacco companies and had a troubling record over race relations. The saying in North Carolina was, "Voting for Jesse Helms is like masturbation; everybody does it, but no one admits to it."

Stephen pulled into the parking lot of the women's prison and, as he walked to the administration building, thought of his first days as a prison chaplain. What a learning curve it had been! He greeted the officer at the metal detector, flashed his photo ID, and walked through into the grounds. Katz's office was a short walk away. As he entered the building, he ran into Kate McIntyre, the other of the two psychologists at the prison.

"Stephen!" she called out cheerily. "We've been missing you since you got sent 'down the hill' and wherever else they send you." They chatted a moment or two and Stephen went to Ben's open door, stepped over the threshold and said, "Nu?"

"Nu. Jesse Helms has just announced a new welfare breakfast plan for school children."

"Which is?"

"A peanut butter sandwich and a pack of Camels. Have a seat. Want some tea?"

"Sure."

"Peppermint?'

"Fine."

Ben Katz was a tea fanatic. He had his tea caddy filled with dozens of flavors from across the globe. Katz went into the hallway to fill the kettle from the water fountain. He looked like a small, forty-something, balding Freud, with the motions and gesticulations of Groucho Marx.

Katz handed Stephen the steaming mug. "*L'khai'im*. So, *hakhol b'seder*?" (Everything okay?)

"Well, not exactly," began Stephen.

"Do we need to close the door?" Stephen nodded.

"Fine. You close it." Katz grinned.

"Cheeky bugger," laughed Stephen as he got up and closed the door. Then, he set out the facts as he knew them, since the night of Jackson's disappearance.

As he listened, Katz swiveled back and forth in his desk chair and tapped a pencil against his palm. As soon as Stephen finished, he took a deep breath and, as he let it out, said, "Not a coincidence." He tapped the eraser on the desk blotter as though emphasizing his point. "Not sure what to make of Ralph Martin, though. Hard to believe he's dirty. But his reaction to you was strange. But it might not be what you think."

"How's that?" queried Travis.

"Well..." Katz began hesitantly, "I would give him a diagnosis—if I knew him better—you understand. But I would say, as an educated guess, that the man is a manic-depressive. That would explain much of the hot-cold relationship you have experienced. It all depends on which day you catch him. I also think he self-medicates." Katz made a drinking motion with his right hand.

"Really?" asked Travis.

"I had the opportunity to spend a few days around Martin a year or two back when we had a retreat for clinical professionals down in the Uwharrie State Park. Morning and evening, Martin had the faint, sweet smell of booze on his breath. I'm not saying he gets sloppy drunk—which he might—but I am saying he hits the bottle more than is healthy." Katz thought for a brief moment and then added, "Especially for a man in his profession—and you know what I mean."

The two men sat in silence for a while. Stephen then pointed at the papers he had brought. "May I ask you to keep these here for me?"

"You certainly may. I will file them under 'W'." Not understanding, Stephen shook his head. "For 'weird shit'," quipped Katz.

~ * ~

That evening Stephen and Emily went for a bike ride, starting at his cottage and winding their way around Raleigh's leafier, inner neighborhoods. After about ten miles, Emily pulled up alongside Stephen and said, "Okay, Buster, spill it!"

Disconcerted, Stephen asked, "What do you mean?"

"Just the fact that we have ridden for forty minutes and you've not spoken a word. What's going on?"

"Oh, I don't know. It's just that I haven't wanted to involve you in my work...I haven't wanted prison to leech over into 'our time'."

"Too late!" puffed Emily. Then indicating with her right hand, "Park bench! Halt and dismount!"

Stephen jokingly saluted Emily and they wheeled over to the side of the road and leaned their road bikes against a tree. Emily plopped herself unceremoniously on the bench. Stephen started to sit down, but then noticed one of his cycling shoes was untied. He bent down on one knee in front of the bench with Emily sitting there, but without thinking about what it looked like.

"Oh my God!" gasped Emily. "Are you proposing to me?!"

Stephen was totally caught off guard, blushed a bright crimson, and stammered, "Um... oh...gosh...no...that is...I mean, if I were to propose, it would certainly be to you...but, uh no, um...oh God!" He hid his face in his hands. Neither of them knew what to say. Stephen took his cycling helmet off and dropped it on the grass. He still couldn't look up. A moment later, he felt Emily's long, cool fingers running through his damp, matted hair. He realized he felt electrified whenever this woman touched him. He also recognized that if he were to marry anyone, he hoped it would be Emily. He had never given this feeling conscious life in words. Damn! Of all the conflicting feelings he could be having—a prison caper and the realization that he was falling in love.

"I'm sorry." Stephen thought he heard a sob. Could Emily be crying? He had admired her strength and forthrightness—from her life's work to her lovemaking. She knew her own mind. He had never seen her cry—for any reason. He ventured to look up and saw tears running down Emily's face. Each started to speak at the same time—stammering and stumbling over their words. Stephen deferred to Emily.

"Can you forgive me? God, I feel so stu-pid! I—"

Stephen hadn't reckoned on Emily feeling as tripped up as he did. He placed his fingers of his right hand gently over Emily's lips. His left index finger he placed over his own, "Shhh. Don't say anything else." He removed his fingers and kissed her, holding it for a long time. He took her face in both hands, and gazed at her, drawing her nearer. Emily's eyes glistened and Stephen felt his burning now as well. "I love you."

"You don't have to say—"

Stephen cut her short again. "I said, 'I—love—you'. You. Emily. You are the woman I love. I just hadn't found the right time—and, as neither of us has uttered the 'L word' so far, well, I was a little scared of being the first...the first to say it—to say 'I love you.' And now that I have, it seems so easy—and so right. Even if you do kick me in the balls."

Emily gave him a shove and he went over onto the grass—laughing. Wiping her eyes, Emily joined in the laughter. Stephen lay there for a time, simply looking at her—almost with new eyes. She returned his gaze and they conversed without words. After a few minutes, Stephen got up from the grass and said, "Let's go home. We can eat and talk." They made it back to the cottage in half the time it had taken them to get to the park bench. They locked the bikes to the iron railing on the steps and went inside. As summer hadn't quite let go of this part of the South, they were both soaked with sweat. Stephen said, "How about we have a shower?" Emily didn't argue.

They entered the small bathroom and stripped off. Although the cottage had no bath, it did have a sizeable shower—perfect for two. They took turns ducking under the refreshing water and washing the salt from their bodies. Then Stephen engaged in what he called 'grooming.' He shampooed Emily's hair and massaged her scalp—something she had come to enjoy about their evening showers.

Stephen had explained that his desire for such grooming came from watching films about Jane Goodall's experiences with chimpanzees. Their grooming of one another built group cohesion. "But to be completely truthful," he had added with a mischievous grin the first time they had showered together, "It's just a flimsy excuse to touch you all over."

Stephen rinsed Emily's hair and applied the conditioner. Each step elicited a low animal-like moan from Emily. She then returned the favor for him. The fun usually began when they washed one another below the shoulders. Emily loved washing Stephen's back and his well-muscled legs. She laughed as she ran the cloth over his thighs. "I have noticed, Reverend, that the more I wash you, the more of you there is to wash! Have you noticed that?" Emily gave him a tug. It was his turn to moan. "You see," she purred, "When I began washing you here, there wasn't that much to wash. Is that fair?"

Being a man, Stephen was already losing his mind and indulging in his senses. Emily nibbled her way up his chest, gave him a lush kiss and turned around. Leaning against the seat in the corner of the shower, she worked Stephen inside her and they made frantic love. His hand did for her what her warm insides did for him and they soon reached that point where knees tend to collapse. Emily spun around and sat on the small seat, gasping for air and laughing. Stephen went to his knees and then plopped himself on his left hip. He lay his head on Emily's thigh, as he felt his heart pounding within his chest.

"There you go again," puffed Emily, "getting on your knees in front of me! Wasn't once enough?" An hour before, they had both been stung with embarrassment; now they could both laugh at themselves—something each treasured about the other without ever having said so. The two lovers savored the moment until the hot water began to run out.

"Yikes," shouted Stephen. "Off! Off! Off!" he spluttered as he got up to turn off the water. He grabbed their towels and they both grinned like Cheshire cats.

"That would have been a real passion killer had it happened a few minutes earlier!" Emily chuckled. She added, "Oh, look! Mr. Wobbly is back!"

Attempting his best impression of Sydney Greenstreet, Stephen responded, "I say Emily, you are quite the card! Upon my word, woman, quite the card!"

He put his hands in Emily's damp hair. "An hour or so ago, I told you that I love you—and it wasn't just words to make you feel better. I meant them—and I mean them. So, how do they sound now? Here we are—naked and unashamed. No secrets. No games."

"They sound like 'home.' That's another four-letter word you used today." Stephen looked at Emily quizzically. "You said to me 'Let's go home.' In the past you've either said—and me too— 'Let's go to your place' or 'Let's go to my place.' And that is how it's been for several months. But today you said, 'Let's go home.' And I came with you because I love you. Being with you feels like home. And that is a new experience for me."

Stephen's eyes filled with tears for the second time that day. "And for me." He opened his arms and enfolded Emily—skin to skin. He couldn't help but think of the verse from the Song of Songs: "I have found the one my soul loves." He kissed Emily's forehead. "How about a homecoming meal?"

"Delighted," came Emily's response. "But I assume we are dressing for the occasion?"

Six

As they prepared dinner together, Emily paused, looked at Stephen and smiled. "What?" he asked.

"Just look at us getting all domestic. Who'd a thunk it six months ago?"

"Well, not I," offered Stephen, "But I ain't complaining either!" He grabbed Emily around the waist and brought their lips together.

After a long kiss, Emily gave Stephen a nibble on the tip of his nose and then a push. "Tired! Hungry! Eat!" He laughed as they went back to their tasks, and he decided it was as good a time as any to open up about recent events at the advancement center.

Once dinner was ready, they carried their meal to the small dining area with its round, wooden table. Emily had learned that Stephen always liked to offer a prayer of thanks before a meal. At first, she found it quaint—something she had not done since childhood—but then she had come to see it as consistent with the person Stephen was, a man who was truly grateful for the basic things in life. She also loved it when he prayed using the Hebrew prayer of thanksgiving: *haMotzi*. It, too, went from being merely exotic to her ears to something which made her think about everything for which she had to give thanks.

They ate for several minutes in silence. It was broken by Emily. "Stephen, I'm glad you shared with me about your work—and your concerns. I know why you don't want your work to invade our time, but...well, it's part of you and now part of 'us'—whatever that might mean for you and me." Wiping her mouth, she changed tack. "Look, I'm really sorry about that 'proposal' malarkey back at the park. I...I felt so stupid, like a schoolgirl. I don't even know what possessed me to say that! I don't usually go for that traditional nonsense."

Stephen lifted his hand for silence. "Shh. It doesn't matter. All is forgiven. In fact, it was probably a good thing." Emily shook her head, uncomprehendingly. "Your 'gaffe' or whatever you want to call it, has helped to throw my feelings for you into high relief—and the fact that there is, well, an 'us-ness'."

Emily laughed at Stephen's neologism. "'Us-ness,' I like that."

"It seems to me that we have somehow crossed some sort of invisible boundary today—invisible because it exists only in our hearts. And we clearly have deep feelings for one another. I've enjoyed how things have developed between you and me—and I suppose I didn't want to think about them too much for fear that maybe this was just a fling for you."

Emily laid her napkin in her lap and looked Stephen straight in the eye. "Far from it." She stopped herself from saying what was in her mind: *Although you are a good fuck!*

"So let me just say this," Stephen continued, "and I don't want to elaborate any further tonight, if you don't mind. But if I were to propose to anyone, it would be you." They both sat with the gravity of what they had just said and heard, Emily honoring Stephen's request.

When the meal was finished and they both began to clear up, Emily asked, "Are you allowed to bring visitors to the prisons where you work?"

"Yes. Are you interested?"

"Why shouldn't I be?" She gave Stephen a hip bump.

"No reason at all," said Stephen. "I can arrange it most any time."

"Good," Emily said succinctly. "And I'd like for you to see some of my work first-hand." And then, with a mischievous look in her eye, "And I might even get you directly involved." She winked.

~ * ~

"I didn't quite expect this," grunted Stephen. "Are you sure this thing will hold the bull?" He was crouched beneath a tubular steel frame with a cow's hide thrown over it.

"It hasn't failed yet," grinned Emily, as she and a farmhand led the bull toward his intended 'mate'. "Just hold the glass beaker where you can catch the semen. You'll figure it out!" Emily laughed heartily at Stephen's predicament.

Nervously, he watched the ton-and-a-half bull entering the enclosure. The thought of being beneath this over-sexed beast who couldn't tell the difference between a real cow and a steel 'surrogate' was unsettling to say the least.

"You know, this isn't exactly what I thought I'd be doing with you in your field work...Watching a bull get his rocks off and with me catching his semen." Was he talking just to calm himself down? Stephen noticed his hand was shaking ever so slightly. Emily was occupied with the bull, so she hadn't responded. But within seconds of his release, the bull was on his steel mate.

Stephen held out the beaker while turning his head aside. It was all over in a matter of seconds and the bull was back on all fours, being led away by his nose ring.

Although there was no need to hurry, Stephen crawled quickly from under the cow manikin and handed the beaker to Emily. She applauded as he approached. "Well done, Reverend! Now we put the goods in a cool box and take it back to the lab." He was happy to hand it over. "That wasn't so bad, was it? After all, you took me on a tour of the advancement center and women's prison."

"Yeah, but I didn't ask you to interact so intimately with the inmates." Stephen rolled his eyes for effect. "So why did we need to do this?"

"Lots of reasons. Breeders need to know about the bull's fertility, sperm motility—whether he can do what he needs to do to keep the herd going." She winked at Stephen. "We also need to be aware of environmental factors which can affect the bull's fertility—as well as the cows. We check for all kinds of things. But my research focuses more on environmental impact on herd animals." They climbed back into the university's pickup truck. "Here," said Emily, "you get to hold the bull juice!" Stephen made a low growl, but still was smiling.

They bumped their way over some tractor ruts as they headed out onto the highway. Emily gave the farm manager a friendly wave as they left. "Just wait until we're back at the labs. I have a treat for you!" She grinned puckishly.

"Hey wait, isn't that what you said about the farm visit?"

"Aw, be a good sport! You get to wear plastic gloves for this one!"

With a nasally deadpan twang, Stephen remarked, "Wow. I can hardly wait." Emily tickled his ribs to get the smile she wanted.

Along the road, they could see the beginnings of autumn's tinges in some of the hardwood trees. "So why didn't you want to become a veterinarian?" Stephen asked.

"Reasonable question." Emily thought for a moment before speaking. "Well, I did, at first. But then my interest is more in identifying and solving problems than in treating them. If that makes sense."

"Yeah, it does. I suppose being a prison chaplain is a bit like being a vet—we deal with people after they've screwed up. I suppose you could be compared to a teacher or social worker who tries to keep the problems from happening."

"Well done, Rev! You get an A for today. I might even let you accompany me to collect some dung next time!" They both laughed as they sped along the way to the university.

~ * ~

Back at the labs, Emily spoke to two of her undergraduate students about tests she wanted them to run on the bull's deposit. She then grabbed Stephen by the hand and led him downstairs into a tiled room where a Jersey cow stood happily eating hay. She was tethered to a ring on the wall. She didn't seem bothered by the two intruders.

"Notice anything different about Felicia?"

Stephen cast his eyes over the bovine and then said, "Well, yeah. She's got some sort of plug in her side."

"That, dear Reverend, is called a fistula. It's a surgically made opening into the cow's rumen—the first of her four stomachs. Thus her name: Felicia the Fistulated cow. Nice, eh?"

"Clever that."

"Want to peek inside?"

"Won't she mind? Seriously?"

"Nah, it's her job. Loads of students have looked in and felt the inside of her rumen—just like you're about to do. Now put

54

these gloves on." Stephen did as he was told while Emily unscrewed the giant plug in Felicia's side. "Here, you might want this." Emily held out a flashlight.

Stephen seemed uncertain. "It's dark inside. Take it!"

Almost gingerly, Stephen clicked on the light and shone it into the cow as she absentmindedly chewed her cud. "Wow—a lot of hay!"

"Yep. Some cows can hold two hundred pounds of grass or hay in their rumens. Have a feel."

Stephen hesitated. "Won't it bother her?"

"Did you feel your breakfast being digested this morning? No. Because there are no nerve endings in the rumen. Come on now, Reverend."

He handed Emily the flashlight and put his hand inside the cow. "Man, it's really warm in here!"

"So is your stomach. Have a feel of the stomach's lining."

"And she can't feel this?"

"Nope. But you can ask her if you like!" Emily grinned at Stephen. "Had enough of a poke around?"

"Yep." Stephen removed his hand and pulled off the gloves. "I assume I won't have further need of these?"

Emily shook her head and led Stephen to a display table with a strange variety of objects: wristwatches, nails, rusted gate hinges, fence wire and more. "Guess where we got these," prompted Emily.

"Haven't a clue," responded Stephen.

"From inside the rumens of cows." Emily watched for Stephen's reaction.

"What?! All of this assorted junk?"

"Every piece. Cows are the true pigs. Pigs are much more discerning. Cows get what we call 'hardware disease.' The problem for cattle is when the metal—or whatever they have swallowed—starts to move through to the reticulum or 'second stomach.' If it is sharp, then it can puncture the lining of the reticulum and enter the peritoneal cavity, causing inflammation. Other times it might even puncture the pericardium or the heart itself, which can lead to death."

"I think I kinda understood most of that," Stephen shook his head. "So what do you do if the cow swallows something metal? Surgery?"

"I'm glad you asked that question, young sir," Emily's eyes twinkled while she hefted what looked like a giant lozenge. "We push this down their throats."

"Which is?"

"A large magnet. It attracts the metal objects and, in theory, keeps them in the bottom of the rumen." Stephen shook his head in amazement.

"Any questions? You know I'll be testing you on this later."

"Only one question. May I kiss you? I don't think Felicia will mind."

Emily cocked her head. "I'm not sure such things are allowed between teacher and student."

"So, keep me after class." Stephen took Emily's face in his hands and planted his lips on hers. Then he drew back and said, "You know, Ms. Webster; you're a potent mixture of woman: athleticism, beauty and brains. Just what I've always wanted."

Emily looked up and nibbled Stephen's chin. "Play your cards right, Rev, and I just might stick around."

Seven

Stephen pulled into the advancement center parking lot feeling lighter than air. The chaplain was in love—completely smitten—unable to think about or do anything for more than five minutes without thinking about Emily. And she loved him too. Several days had passed since their momentous bike ride, when they had confessed their feelings for each other. So far, nothing that the North Carolina Department of Corrections had thrown at him had been able to deflate his buoyant mood.

James Fowler was on the front desk this morning. Stephen gave him a cheery grin and a wave as he entered and turned to go to his office. "Hey man," called Fowler. "Where's the fire? Let me talk atcha for a minute."

Stephen stopped in his tracks and turned to James. "What's up?"

"You are, my man. I haven't ever seen you so energized and bouncy. What's her name?"

"That obvious, is it?"

"For folks who have eyes."

Stephen looked around to make certain no one was in ear shot. "Emily's her name. And we've been seeing each other for about five months. She's a grad student at NC State. I couldn't design a better woman for me! She's incredible."

James' face lit up for Stephen. "Man, that's wonderful. I'm really happy for you. When do I get to meet her?"

"Well funnily enough I brought her here a few weeks back— and to the women's prison—just to show her where I work. Unfortunately, it was your day off."

"Well I hate I missed her. What have you got planned for Thanksgiving?"

"Nothing yet. Why?"

"How about you two come over to my house and eat the big bird with Diane, me and the kids?"

"I'd like that, James. I'll ask Emily this evening. Thanks."

As Stephen turned to go, James added, "Oh, Levon Davis wants to see you. Told him I'd let you know." Fowler hesitated a moment and then added, "Have you heard about Walter Jackson?"

"No, why?"

"He's dead."

"No! What happened?"

"He died of a gunshot wound. Seems his body was found in an abandoned tenant farm house, barely ten miles from his home. He'd been there for some time, because some kids who were playing near the house could smell the stench from his body. They decided to peek inside the house and...well, you can imagine what they saw. Anyway, they took off—scared shitless, I guess—and one of their parents called the sheriff. As there was a warrant out for Jackson, they contacted the corrections department." Nodding at the warden's office, James continued, "Harris got the report this morning. Most everybody here knows about it now."

Travis stood in front of Fowler, dumfounded. "You okay?" asked James.

"I don't know—yeah, maybe. No, not really." And then *sotto voce* Travis said to Fowler, "Can we go to my office for a minute?" At the same time, both men looked back at the other staff offices. James nodded to Stephen and they made a move to Stephen's office.

Once inside his office, Stephen quietly closed the door, and before either of the men could sit, Stephen whispered, "James, you've gotta be thinking what I'm thinking."

"Gun shots on the night that Jackson took off?"

"Absolutely! How did Harris seem to you when he broke the news about Jackson?"

"More nervous than usual maybe. But when one or two of us tried to ask questions, he cut us short. Basically told us that it's case closed."

"Well it's not closed for me," interjected Stephen. "As the chaplain here, I have a duty and a right to contact the family."

James nodded his head thoughtfully and added, "Just make sure you be careful. There's some weird shit going down around here."

"Will do. I won't say anything to Harris. I'll just go look at Jackson's file in Maxine's office."

"Well, you better do it soon. Jackson's records will be going to the head office later today or early tomorrow."

Stephen let Fowler leave and get back to his desk before going to the front office himself. He consciously walked as quietly as possible and tried not to be in too great a hurry. Harris was on the phone when Stephen passed by his open door. The next door was Maxine's where all of the center's files were kept. "Good morning, Maxine. How's it going?" he asked.

"Just fine and dandy, Chaplain. How 'bout yew?" came her reply in full Tammy Wynette intonation.

"Happy as a dead pig in the sunshine," replied Stephen. Maxine let out an owl-like hoot of laughter as he quickly leafed through the file folder for Walter Jackson. "Just getting some info I need." He pulled a pen from his shirt pocket and made some quick notes, all the while keeping his back toward Maxine.

"Need inny he'p, Chaplain?"

"No, thank you, Maxine. Got all I need. Must go!" Stephen did not want to get pulled into a conversation with Maxine—not to mention Harris or any other officers who might be around.

"Well, bye," called Maxine as Stephen swiftly walked back to his office.

Once at his desk, Stephen started to call Jackson's family two or three times, but each time put the phone back on its cradle. He was aware that he was beginning to feel a bit paranoid about pursuing Jackson's death—and its circumstance—from his office telephone. What if? Just what if the line is tapped? Before he could make up his mind, he heard a gentle knock on his door. Something told him not to call out 'Come in' but to get up and open the door himself, which he did. Levon Davis was standing there—as close to the door as he could get without merging with the wood.

"Oh, Levon, yeah, man I forgot to come find you. Come on in."

Levon edged his way inside before Stephen had fully opened the door. "Yeah, well at least I found you. Rev, man I'm glad to see you!" Levon's eyes searched the day room and then down the corridor one last time before closing the door behind him. Travis noticed that Davis' shirt had an unusual bulge in it. As soon as he had sat down, Levon unfastened the top two buttons on his shirt. "Marvin tole me he gave you some of Jackson's papers and you got 'em safely hid—right?"

"Yes, that's right."

"Well, put these with 'em." Davis looked at the door—as though there might be someone behind it.

"May I have a look first?" queried Stephen.

"Yeah, yeah, man, go ahead, but let's make it quick, okay? You've heard about Jackson, right?" Levon was clearly worried. "I don't wanna be next."

Once more Stephen found himself staring at a handwritten bill of sale, not unlike the one Marvin Jacobs had brought him a few weeks back. But instead of Thelma Jackson's name on it, it had Irene Davis' name—Levon's mother. Stephen looked underneath and found three more—all with different names of residents' family members on them. They also had what looked like the same name badly written on them: Vance Strader. Levon was silent while Stephen looked over the documents.

When Stephen looked up, Davis was rubbing his chin nervously. "You see what's going on?" he asked the chaplain.

"Well, I think so," said Stephen slowly and deliberately. "It looks like your mother and several others have bought used cars from a Vance Strader—is that right?"

"Right, and you know whose brother he be?"

Stephen slowly looked up at Levon and then unconsciously at the front offices.

"Yeah, damn straight! And you know as well as me and all the others, that this shit is against all prison regulations."

Stephen began to feel as though an elephant had hitched a ride on his back. He reached for his chair in order to guide himself to the seat without collapsing. Without looking up, he said, "This thing is big. Really big."

61

"The thing is, preacher man," Levon spoke firmly, but in an avuncular fashion, "what're you gonna do about it?"

Stephen lifted his gaze to meet Levon's. "My problem is that I don't know whom to trust. I will tell you that I went to Ralph Martin, the head of chaplaincy services, after Jackson disappeared. Frankly, he wasn't interested. But there is one person in the system I know I can trust."

"Who's that?" asked Davis.

"Best you don't know—at least at this point in time. But let me ask you one question for clarification: How many people in the advancement center does this involve—do you know?"

"Let's just say it was everybody who didn't go runnin' outside the night we heard the gunfire. They pretty well knew what was going on."

Stephen whistled softly to himself. Then quickly rose to his feet. "I've gotta get these documents out of here—I have a safe place for them. Don't worry."

Levon simply nodded and then said, "I'm gone." As he opened the office door, he stopped, looked over his shoulder and said, "Be careful, Rev."

Stephen picked up his car keys. His mind was racing as he started to leave his office, but then he remembered the documents. He dug around in the desk drawer and brought out one of the large, inter-office mail envelopes, hastily shoved the paperwork into the envelope and began to make his way to the front. At that moment, Marvin Jacobs sprang into mind. Stephen exited the back door of the center and went to the weight-training area where he opened the covered box where weights were kept. He was surprised to find they were all in order. Stephen cast his eyes around the yard and at the building. No one was watching. He picked up one of the two-and-a-half-pound weights and walked, as nonchalantly as possible, to the picnic table, where he placed it on the corner. Stephen then went around behind the building to access his car in the parking lot.

~ * ~

Fifteen minutes later, Stephen was in the waiting area outside the psychologists' and social workers' offices at the women's prison. Ben was at the coffee urn with his colleague, Kate McIntyre.

"Well, if it isn't our renegade rabbi!" Then, in Katz's *non sequitur* fashion, he launched into a joke. "So a rabbi, a priest and a minister always play a round of golf on Friday mornings. But on this particular day the group of four who are playing ahead of them, are complete duffers. They can barely tee-off—missing the ball seven or eight times—and when they do connect, the ball dribbles off the tee. They tear the green up with their clubs and never replace the turf from the divots they create. Well, the three clergymen could only take so much, so they start making their feelings known to the group. They start to express their anger, cursing out loud and leaving no doubt as to their feelings. And worse, they won't let the three clergymen play through. Well, this goes on for the entire eighteen holes. They barely have time to get back to the clubhouse for a drink before the rabbi needs to prepare for shabbat. While they are at the bar, they see the club's pro passing by, so they call him over. They tell him of their disgust at these most unprofessional and discourteous golfers who held them up all day. The pro gasps, covers his mouth and says, 'Oh my God, I forgot to tell you. Those golfers are blind!' Upon hearing that, the priest says, 'I can't believe how rude I was to them. It was so unworthy of my calling. I must go make my confession.' The minister was shaking his head and decrying his behavior, and said, 'I have to re-write Sunday's sermon. I need to let my flock know just how unchristian I am.' Meanwhile the rabbi said nothing, so his two colleagues say to him, 'What about you? What do you think about it all?'

'What do I think? Why couldn't they have played at night?'" Both Stephen and McIntyre doubled up with laughter.

Without missing a beat, Ben nodded at the manila envelope in Stephen's hand. "Is that what I think it is?"

"More than likely."

They both apologized to Kate about leaving her alone. Katz motioned to Stephen, "To the *kodesh kodashim*."

Kate looked puzzled. Stephen smiled and translated for her: "The holy of holies." He and Ben disappeared behind the closing door.

Stephen handed the envelope to Ben and asked him to take a look at its contents. Katz rubbed his balding head as he was wont to do when concentrating. "So someone in the advancement center is selling used cars to the inmates—or their families?"

"That's what it looks like," agreed Stephen. "But the guard we have at the center is named Melvin Strader, so Vance appears to be his brother. But there's more."

"More?" Ben leveled his gaze on Stephen. "Go on."

"The guy who ran off weeks back—Walter Jackson?—well he was found dead this week. He died of a gunshot wound."

Ben stood and started pacing the floor. "Who else knows about this?"

"I'm not sure, beyond the guys caught up in it. And there are more of them than the number of documents in your hand. I heard it today from one of the guys whose bill of sale is in the envelope. Oh—I did go to Ralph Martin about the gunfire, but he tore me a new A-hole for going outside the chain of command. Which, as a matter of fact, I didn't do; but that didn't matter to him. He told me it was none of my business and to let it go."

"Ralph told you to 'let it go,' eh? But you can't, can you?"

"Hell no!' blurted Stephen. "My pastoral concern for these guys extends to their families as well."

Ben nodded with approval. "That's my rabbi. And neither should you let it go—that's what the system has done for most of our inmates." Katz stopped his pacing as an idea came to him. "Don't go back to Ralph Martin unless you must, okay?" Stephen agreed.

"What you need to do is cover your *tuchas*. And you do that by putting your concerns into writing. Make sure I get a copy." Ben resumed his pacing, but more slowly. With each pace he made a statement. "Tell you what. Let's photocopy all of the documents we have so far. I'll keep the originals at home and a copy here. You take a copy home as well and send a copy to Martin, with your regards—but no letter. And then we wait to see what happens."

Stephen thought, *Does Katz realize he has switched from 'you' to 'we?'* In any case, the change of pronouns buoyed Stephen. He had an ally. "Do you think Martin might be in on this in some way?" he asked.

Ben started to speak, but checked himself. "I would like to think Martin isn't involved. But after the shenanigans your predecessor, Chaplain Goodman, got up to with the female inmates, I wouldn't want to venture a guess about Martin. But we can't rule him out. Give me some more time to consider what we do after we have heard from Ralph Martin."

"Oh—I forgot to mention. I plan to go to Walter Jackson's funeral. I might be able to get some more information from them, if they are willing to talk about it."

Katz nodded enthusiastically. "Right. Let's get these documents photocopied. Actually, you'd better wait here. I'll take them up to the admin building for copying.

"Hey, Ben?"

Ben turned as he was going out the door. "Yeah?"

"I'm glad you're on board with me."

"*Al lo davar.*"

Eight

The gravel in the Holiness Church's parking lot crunched as Stephen pulled in. He laughed, given that the church was named after the town, Turkey. Who named so many of the towns in this state: Speed, Salvo, Lizard Lick, and Turkey? he mused. The chaplain noticed there weren't many cars. He pondered the fact that Jackson had spent nearly three decades behind bars. Who remembered him? His wife or siblings?—if he had any. Stephen had worn his clerical collar and ID to help the family members know who this interloper was. When he entered the rustic, wooden church building, he saw a number of people standing beside the coffin. *Thank heaven it's closed*, Stephen thought. He walked up to the small group and introduced himself. Before the service began, a small, heavily weathered woman introduced herself as Thelma Jackson, Walter's widow. She seemed pleased that someone had come from the last unit in which her husband had lived. Stephen was invited back to her house following the service for a gathering, and he accepted the invitation.

The service was short and sad. The minister hadn't known Walter, so left it to a few family members to share some memories. Jackson's coffin was carried outside for burial in the church cemetery. Stephen stood a short distance away from the family and the few friends who were in attendance. Following the interment, people drifted back to their cars. Stephen had a few words with Thelma. She indicated the car she had been brought in and told him to follow them back to her house. Stephen was glad to do so, as he would have had no idea how to get there. Two of the roads were no more than gravel tracks. The cars ahead of him pulled into a driveway with a somewhat dilapidated farmhouse at the end. The barn looked as though it would cave in at any minute. The half-dozen cars parked higgledy-piggledy under the bare pecan trees.

Stephen made his way up the rickety steps to the porch. Thelma held the door open for him. The front room reminded him of homes some of his older relatives lived in along the slopes of the Blue Ridge Mountains. There was a large oil heater in front of the unused fire place. The floor covering was a floral-patterned linoleum, which made a crackling sound as he walked over it. Stephen picked up the slight smell of kerosene, which fueled the heater. On one of the walls was a shelf with a photograph of Walter, smiling in his Second World War uniform, and a picture of him with other soldiers somewhere in Europe. Next to the photos was what looked like a German Luger pistol.

"Walter served during the last war—from D-Day until VE Day." The man introduced himself as Thelma's brother, Roy McNair, and offered his hand. Despite his wiry frame, he had the strong grip of a farmer or someone who had done years of manual labor. Roy pointed to a chair and invited Stephen to sit. Pointing at the pistol, Roy added, "Walter took that gun off a German officer he captured." He cleared his throat and in soft tones said, "We—Thelma and me—would like to ask you some questions about the last weeks of Walter's life. We ain't had much information to speak of."

"I'll tell you what I can," responded Stephen.

"Thelma and her cousins'll be bringing food out here in a minute. Hope you'll stay and eat."

"Thank you. It's very kind." No sooner had he spoken than Thelma and company were bringing out covered dishes with fried chicken, potato salad, green beans and corn bread. True Southern fare. Roy set up a card table on which the food was placed.

"Chaplain Travis," enquired Roy, "would you be willing to say grace?"

Stephen stood and spoke. "Lord God, we're gathered here at a very sad time. Walter should have been here, sharing a homecoming meal, after too many years in prison. We pray that he is with us in spirit and comfort for his wife and friends. Finally, we ask your blessings on the food we eat and the hands that have prepared it." Amens echoed around the room.

Thelma took Stephen by the arm and directed him to the food. "We serve preachers and guests first around here. Don't be shy."

Stephen took a plate and served himself a little of everything. By the time he was back to his chair, Thelma was there with a glass of iced tea. Once everyone had filled a plate, Roy turned to Thelma and said, "Sister, the rever'nd says he'll share news about Walter."

"That would be helpful, Rever'nd Travis, 'cause the prison system and the police ain't tole us nothing much. But let's wait until everybody's eaten."

69

The meal was a somber affair, with people chatting in twos and threes. After about forty-five minutes, most of the well-wishers had left. At that point, one of Thelma's cousins went into the kitchen to wash the dishes.

Thelma directed her attention to Stephen. "How do you figger Walter come to be shot? And who done it? Because the police ain't caught nobody."

"Well Thelma, hang on a minute, 'cause I think we first wanna know why he run. He was due to be released purt' soon. Isn't that right, Rever'nd?"

Stephen wiped his mouth with a napkin and then took a sip of tea, giving himself time to think.

He felt deeply for these country folks, who had obviously been fobbed off by the powers that be. Stephen took a deep breath and released it slowly. He prayed silently, *Give me the words, Lord.* Measuring what he would say, knowing they deserved the truth, he began. "Has anyone told you about the night Walter disappeared from the advancement center?" They shook their heads. "Walter had been seen at the center that evening. He had come in from work, showered and then had his supper with the other residents. After supper, most of the men were in the day room watching the Ali/Spinks fight. During that time, most of us heard what sounded like gunfire coming from behind the building." Stephen saw the look of surprise from Thelma and Roy.

"Gunfire!? Ain't nobody tole us anything about gunfire at the center!" spat Thelma.

Stephen studied all the faces silently, waiting for him to continue. He realized he was biting his lower lip. "I think I could be in a lot of trouble for what I am telling you. I hope it's not too late to ask you not to reveal where you got this information because, like you, I want to get to the bottom of this. I promise to get back to you when I know more. I swear it. I hate to ask it, but can I trust you not to say where you've learned these things?"

Roy spoke up first. "As long as you give us the truth, Rever'nd. We'll protect you." Stephen took notice of the word 'protect.' He wondered whether he would indeed require protection—and from whom?

"First, may I ask you what you were told about Walter's leaving the advancement center?"

"Only that they reckon he got rabbit in him and took off," said Roy. "They said a lot of convicts git real nervous before they's released. We was told a lot of men don't know how to make it outside of prison after years behind bars—so they do something just so's they'll git sent back to prison."

Stephen caught himself biting his lower lip again. An uneasy feeling was growing within him. "Who told you that?"

Both Thelma and Roy spoke at the same time: "Warden Harris."

"Do you two think Walter was worried about being released?"

"Not one teeny bit," blurted Thelma. "Walter was calling me regular, and when I could git up there to see 'im, he was fine.

Stephen nodded his assent and continued. "I agree with you. I heard nothing from Walter which suggested to me that he was worried about his release. As far as I knew, he was looking forward to being back here with you." Stephen paused to collect his thoughts. "I want to share with you what I know from the night Walter left the center. I was in my office when I heard two shots. It sounded like a handgun. Officer James Fowler was first on the scene and said he smelled cordite, from the gunpowder—and that was only seconds after the shots were heard. He and I then searched the grounds, but couldn't find anyone there or any shell casings."

"Probably a revolver," opined Roy.

"Officer Fowler thought the same. I asked the desk officer, Melvin Strader, if he had heard or seen anything—" Stephen broke off when he saw a look of recognition cross Thelma's and Roy's faces.

"Strader? Is that what you said?" asked Thelma. She looked at her brother Roy without saying anything. Meanwhile there were murmurs from others.

Do you recognize that name?" asked Stephen.

"Does he have a brother named Vance?" In his mind's eye, Stephen could see the almost child-like, scrawled name: Vance Strader.

"He might. I don't know for sure."

"Well Roy and I think he does! He approached us a few months back, when Roy was irrigating my corn crop, saying he knows my husband's in prison and how would I like a car to be able to visit him. I said I couldn't afford no car. Roy's been helping look after me and this farm for nearly thirty years now, but even then I'm just scrapin' by. How'm I gonna afford a car? And that's what I tole 'im." Thelma switched her gaze to Roy, as if asking permission to continue. Stephen noticed a slight nod from Roy. "Well, that warn't good enough for Mr. Vance Strader. He said he had a brother worked in the prison system and that he knew Walter. Said it would be a terrible thing if Walter didn't get visited more regular. Said Walter might do something crazy and git hisse'f sent back to the prison farm. Then he points outside to the car he come here in and says to me, 'This here Ford is only six hunnerd dollars.' Then he said, 'What's six hunnerd dollars compared to not seeing my Walter for another four or five years?'"

Stephen noticed that his heart was racing and his stomach was feeling queasy. "So what did you do?"

"Well it become clear to me and Roy that if we didn't buy that car, Walter'd be sent back to Odum farm." She ummed to herself and smoothed the non-existent wrinkles from her dress. "So we done what he asked. Took nearly all of my savings and some of Roy's too." Roy nodded slowly. "Damn thing broke down on my first drive to Fairborn—sorry, Rever'nd." Raising her arm, she pointed outside and said, "And that's the piece of junk sittin' right out there!" Stephen looked out the window to an old, dusty Ford. "Hasn't moved since the day Roy helped tow me back. The transmission is shot to hell and back!"

'So what happened after that?"

"After that? Well, I called Walter and tole 'im what had happened. He said he'd try to fix it by talking with your Mr. Strader. And your fellar Strader said it warn't nothin' to do with 'im! He got to take it up with his brother down here in Sampson County." Thelma's blood was up. "Fat chance o' that! Officer Strader knowed damn well," Travis waved away the swear word so she could continue, "that Walter warn't gonna git permission to come down here—even though he did ask the warden."

"He asked Warden Harris?" interjected Stephen.

"Sho' 'nuff he did! For all the damn good it did!"

"When did he speak with Harris?"

"The week before he run off." Stephen felt himself collapse back in his chair. His mind was spinning.

Trying to control his voice, Stephen asked, "Did Walter ever mention other inmates who were involved in the car buying scheme?" Both Thelma and Roy turned to look at each other and Stephen recognized that the people were weighing up whether they could trust him. It was Roy who spoke first.

"Rever'nd, Walter tole us that about a third of the men in your advancement center had their families pushed into buying cars by Vance Strader."

Stephen covered his face with his hands and leaned forward onto his knees. "Good God Almighty," he mumbled. No one spoke for several minutes. He was glad he had come to visit Jackson's family in his own car. Had he used a state car, he would have had to say exactly where he was going and provide the mileage. As far as he knew, no one at the advancement center, apart from Fowler, knew he was there. But for how long? Stephen fished in his jacket pocket for a small note pad he carried, and then pulled a pen from the inside pocket. "I'm giving you my home telephone number. Only ever call me there. Understood? I have an answering machine if I'm out, so leave me a message." Both Roy and Thelma simply nodded. "Good. Now I need your number too, Roy—that is, if you don't mind? Thelma's was in Walter's file." While Roy was writing it down, Stephen said to both sister and brother, "I think we're all gonna need to keep an eye out for anyone or anything unusual. And certainly, please let me know if you hear from Vance Strader again." When that was all agreed, Stephen said his goodbyes and went out to his car.

~ * ~

On the drive back to Fairborn, Stephen thought back to the night of the shooting. Melvin Strader had claimed not to have heard anything. He hadn't even got up from his seat to see what all the commotion was in the day room, leaving everything to Fowler. Suppose Jackson had gone to speak with Strader while everyone else was concerned with the boxing that night. Maybe the conversation between Jackson and Strader went bad and Walter had been threatened with being returned to Odum prison farm? But wait a minute! Walter had already given his bill of sale to Marvin Jacobs—so he must have known he was on thin ice with Strader. Had he tried to make one more plea with Strader, hoping against hope that he would return the money for the clapped-out car that had been sold to him and his wife?

Nine

When Stephen got back to his office late in the afternoon, Lincoln was in. He smiled and greeted Stephen and then said, "Oh, Marvin Jacobs stopped by a while ago. Says he wants to see you." Stephen remembered the weight he had placed on the picnic table.

"Yeah, thanks, Linc. Did he say where he'd be?"

"He'll be in the day room probably. If not, maybe at the weights." Parker was concentrating on a form he was filling in.

Stephen trusted Lincoln, but didn't know whether he should share what he knew about Jackson's disappearance and death. One thing was certain, he wanted and needed to tell James Fowler. As an African-American, Fowler had felt more than a little let down by the way Warden Harris seemed to kowtow to Melvin Strader and several other white guards. With Jackson dead, Stephen wondered how Harris must be feeling about his white 'guardians.' Stephen decided to keep the circle of knowledge small for the present. First, he would see Marvin and then he would catch up with Fowler.

Marvin Jacobs was out in the exercise yard watching a few colleagues lifting weights. He gave a casual nod to Stephen as he approached where Marvin was sitting. "Afternoon, Mr. Jacobs." Looking at the men who were lifting, Travis said, "You're not joining in?"

"Nah, man," retorted Jacobs, "I had enough lifting in the warehouse where I work. Now I'm just watching." Marvin was flipping the two-and-a-half-pound weight as he talked. "Where you been, Preacher Man?"

Travis looked around before he spoke, and in a low voice said, "Attending Walter Jackson's funeral."

It was clear that Jacobs had a hard time not letting his face show shock or surprise. But his voice remained cool. "Mmh-hmm. And how did it go, Rev?" Marvin slipped easily from the table, stretched and made it look like he simply fancied a walk. Stephen fell in alongside him.

"Let's just say I heard a lot more than I ever wanted to know. This thing with Strader is...well, I don't know how to put it, but it's far-reaching—and dangerous." Upon hearing that, Marvin had to stifle a chuckle.

"Now you learning. You see what we been livin' with all this time. That mutha-fucker Melvin Strader git his brother to do the arm-twisting and paperwork, and he do the threatening or fixing it so us so-called convicts git our asses sent back to finish out our sentences. And they ain't a godammned thing we can do about it." Marvin spat for emphasis. "Strader got them crackers on the staff to fall in with him." Marvin looked at Stephen and said, "Hey, sorry man."

"Don't worry about me, Marvin. "They are a bunch of redneck crackers."

"You know," continued Marvin, "now that Jackson got hisse'f shot, ain't many of the men gonna want to talk about this thing." Jacobs stopped walking and looked straight at Travis. "You gonna be kinda alone with it. How that make you feel?" Stephen knew this to be a test of character. He knew in that instant that what he did or did not do in response to what he knew would be a defining moment for him—and a determining factor as to how well he might sleep every night hence.

Stephen answered Marvin's questions with a question of his own. "Are you still willing to work with me?"

Still holding his gaze, Jacobs said, "Do what I can, Rev."

"Then I will do everything in my power to bring this to light and to justice. Just give me time, okay?"

"Jackson's death done give you time! Hell, every man in here whose family bought a car off the Strader brothers is for sure gonna pay up—at least for now." He laughed sardonically.

"Tell me something, Marvin. What's your gut feeling about Parker? Do you guys trust him?"

Marvin nodded slowly, "GQ? Yeah, he cool."

"It's just that I might need some more inside help before I find out who we can trust. I know I can trust Fowler."

"Well, I wouldn't go no further than them two. And Harris," Marvin spat again, "that nigger ain't nothing but Strader's stooge." Showing concern, Marvin took Stephen's arm. "You ain't said nothing to him, have you?"

"No. Nothing! The only thing I asked him about was Jackson's disappearance and the gunshots. Even then it was clear he didn't want to hear any more about it. I suppose Melvin and his crew warned him off it."

"More 'n likely," mused Marvin. Jacobs then looked all around him and up at the sky. He yawned as he looked back at Stephen. "Ain't you got something to do in your office?" Stephen took the hint and headed back into the building.

~ * ~

Stephen had supper that evening at Emily's shared house. It had been Pat's turn to cook and she had prepared a huge pan full of what she called 'autumn stew.' Charles laughed and called it, 'the week-in-review-stew,' as everything they had left over in the fridge had gone into it. Still they all seemed to find it tasty. Pat had also baked some corn bread, so they enjoyed spooning the stew and dipping their corn bread in it.

"Hey, sweet buns, you're awfully quiet tonight." Charles found it hard not to let Stephen know he had seen him in the buff.

"Yeah, sorry. But I'm afraid it's one of those situations I really can't talk about." Stephen went back to eating.

"Oh, come on! Who're we gonna tell?" came Charles' retort.

"Leave him alone!" Everyone started at Pat's outburst. "Can't you see he doesn't want to talk about it? Why do you extraverted types feel the need to intrude into our space?" Stephen found it both interesting and heartwarming that geeky Pat had included him in her introverted world and felt the need to protect him.

Caught off-guard and feeling abashed, Charles immediately apologized to Stephen—and Pat. "Sorry guys, I sometimes don't realize when I'm being intrusive with my gay ways. I've come to think of us as sort of patchwork family. I'm sorry if I offended you."

"Apology accepted, Charles. We don't care if you're gay. We take you as you are, and your humor is appreciated—most of the time—but sometimes it's best to let things lie."

"Ditto," was all Pat added, except she got up and gave Charles a sideways hug. An amazing gesture from someone who was more than likely on the high end of the autism spectrum.

Charles raised his eyebrows at Stephen and Emily. They smiled warmly and then helped clear away the dishes.

~ * ~

Once Emily and Stephen had repaired to her room, she kissed Stephen and asked, "Can you share with me?"

"You—absolutely!" He tried to smile but it felt more like a grimace.

"Lie down, Stephen, and take some deep breaths." Stephen kicked off his shoes and did just that. Emily joined him and leaned on her hand, looking down on her beloved.

Stephen blinked a few times and took several deep breaths, letting them out slowly. He looked at Emily and said, "I think I'm sitting on a time bomb." Then he began to let out the entire sordid tale regarding Jackson and the Strader brothers.

Having listened without interruption, Emily spoke. "So you're saying that these Strader brothers are willing to kill in order to protect their illicit business?"

Stephen nodded and simply said, "'Fraid so." He thought for a moment and then added, "Another reason I didn't say anything over supper was that I didn't want to alarm Charles and Pat. If the Straders find out I know what's been going on, well...there's just no telling what they might do. They have Warden Harris wrapped around their little fingers. And, well, I have no idea where Ralph Martin comes down on this. I haven't even heard from him since Jackson's death was announced—and he knows that shots were fired at the advancement center. Shit!"

Emily stroked Stephen's head, not with condescension, but with true compassion. "Look, Stephen, you have Katz working with you—and Officer Fowler. That's something. Is it time to open up to Lincoln—at least to feel out where he is with regard to everything?"

"Probably so. Otherwise sharing an office with him will be difficult. It's odd that none of the residents has said anything about Linc. I'll bring it up tomorrow."

Emily and Stephen lay on the bed chatting until they were tired enough to sleep. Around midnight Emily gently shook him. Dazed with REM sleep, he asked, "Um, what?"

"You were having a nightmare," Emily said gently. "You were thrashing about."

"Sorry. I kept seeing Walter Jackson's face; but every time I tried to talk to him, blood came out of his mouth and then he toppled over. Then I heard Melvin Strader's coarse laughter. He never appeared in the dream. Thanks for waking me."

"You gonna be okay?"

"Yeah, I think so. Let's cuddle."

Emily lay her head on Stephen's chest and he entwined her in his arms.

~ * ~

Stephen awoke shortly after dawn. He didn't rush to get up, but lay there listening to the dawn chorus outside and Emily's easy breathing. Stephen's thoughts were mixed with prayers—thanking God for the gift of Emily and praying for guidance regarding the dirty business at the advancement center. He smiled inwardly as Emily began to stir, musing about how her skin was almost indistinguishable from his. The biblical phrase from Genesis came into mind: "And the two shall become one flesh." *So this is how it feels?*

Emily yawned and stretched. "Morning, Reverend. Have you been awake long?"

"Not really. Just enjoying lying here and listening to you breathe."

"Easily amused, aren't you?" Emily gently poked Stephen in the ribs and then kissed him. "Did you sleep well after your nightmare?"

"Must have. I don't remember anything after you woke me."

"Are you going into the advancement center today?"

"Yeah. I think you were right about Linc. I'll try to speak with him today—and Fowler. I want to catch him up on what I know. What about you today? Milking any bulls?"

Emily poked Stephen again in the ribs, "Funny man, eh?" She yawned and stretched. "Lab work today. Mad scientist stuff."

They both arose, cleaned up and had breakfast. Charles and Pat had already left for their respective post-grad work. Before Stephen left, Emily took both of his hands, looked into his eyes and said, "Be careful, won't you?"

"Believe me, I'll do my best. Supper at the cottage tonight?"

"Wouldn't miss it."

~ * ~

As Stephen walked from his car to the entrance to the advancement center, his legs felt somewhat wooden. He dreaded the thought that Melvin Strader might be on the front desk. Stephen felt conspicuous—as though he had 'I know what you're up to' printed on this forehead. His spirits fell when he saw Melvin through the glass door, so Stephen tried to put on his best poker face—the trouble was, he didn't play poker. "Good morning, Melvin. How's it going?"

"Morning, Chaplain. It's going."

Neither man having anything more to say, Stephen went straight to his office. Lincoln was talking with one of the newer residents about a job interview. Stephen gave both of them a nod and proceeded to play with paperwork as he couldn't focus on anything except the Jackson affair. When the new arrival left, Stephen decided to jump right in. "Got a few minutes, Linc?"

"Sure. What's up?"

Stephen got up and closed the door. "It's serious then?" said Lincoln.

'Yeah, very. I need to talk with you about this whole Jackson business. Have you heard much from the guys here?"

Lincoln seemed to twitch a bit before he spoke. "Not much. But it's not good." It seemed that both men were waiting for the other to make a disclosure before he spoke again.

"I went to Jackson's funeral—and spoke with his family."

"Why don't we get some fresh air?" asked Parker, as he reached for his jacket.

They walked out into the autumnal air and sat at the picnic table by the exercise yard. Stephen once more found himself biting his lower lip—it was becoming a habit. "Are you aware, Linc, that Strader and his brother have been putting pressure on the guys to buy used cars from them?"

"Yeah, yeah I am aware. I just wasn't sure what you knew. Shit gets back to Strader, you know."

Travis nodded and then took the scariest leap yet. "I think Strader shot Jackson. So does Walter's wife and her brother."

Parker's face became stone. "I was afraid of that. That's why I've been trying to get my ass transferred outta here. I haven't liked it one little bit since I got here and found out that Uncle Tom Harris is in Strader's pocket."

"You're planning to leave?" Travis was taken aback.

"Look, Stephen, even Fowler has come up against Strader—and the rest of the white officers. As he and I are the only *real* black staff in this place, neither of us has felt...well, safe. You've been a welcome break from these rednecks and I'm aware that the residents have been coming to you. Hell, it's been obvious, 'cause when you aren't here, they've been asking when you'll be in. The thing is, man, the residents that are under Strader's thumb will know that, too." Lincoln instinctively looked around and then added, "You had better watch your back."

Stephen had that heavy feeling once more. "Yeah, I've begun to recognize that."

"Do you carry?" queried Lincoln. "I mean, I know you're a chaplain and all that, but this thing is getting serious."

"I guess I hadn't thought about going that far. I've never liked the idea of owning a handgun. It doesn't fit too well with the teachings of Mr. Jesus."

"Well, all I'm saying is you need to think about it. I have a wife and a baby on the way. I ain't letting those Klansmen in prison uniforms take that away from me."

Travis took solace in the fact that both he and Parker were in agreement about the rot in their workplace. He couldn't blame Linc for wanting to get out—in fact, Stephen felt the same way, but he knew he couldn't leave before seeing the Strader business to the end. Unlike Parker, he had no wife or child. Not that he was keen about getting shot, but his moral compass was incapable of letting the Strader brothers prey on inmates under his care.

And then an idea hit. "Linc, when's the last time there was an open-house for the inmates' families?"

Parker tapped his pencil for a moment and then said, "About twelve to fourteen months ago. We had a softball game and picnic. Why?"

"It occurs to me that if we had, say, an open house before Christmas, we could get a chance to mingle with all of the families who have been hassled into buying a car from the Straders."

Lincoln thought long and hard before he replied. "It's dangerous—but it could work. If we get Fowler to help us, then it wouldn't fall to just one of us to speak to all of the families. Strader might get suspicious."

As with Ben Katz, Stephen noted that Lincoln had said "we."

"Does that mean you're willing to help?"

"Reluctantly, yes. And besides, I can't leave a white guy like you by himself to shuck the jive with the brothers' families, now can I? Look, Rev, I have to get out and visit possible job sites for some of the men. Can you put James in the picture?"

"Can do. And if each of us can speak to the men who have disclosed to us, they can let their families know what we're trying to do."

Parker picked up his jacket and briefcase and then turned again to Travis. "Oh—and you, James and I need to meet somewhere away from this joint and soon."

"Let's make it my place. We can arrange a time after I have spoken with James."

Lincoln departed and Stephen set out to find Fowler. As it transpired, James found him first. "Hey, Stephen, got a few minutes?"

"For you, I have." They shook hands. "Good to see you, James. My office?"

"It's the only safe one around here," replied James, looking over his shoulder as they went in.

"Your timing is perfect," opened Stephen. "I've just had a frank discussion with Lincoln about the Jackson business. Everything keeps leading back to Strader. James, are you aware of the car business he and his brother have been doing with the residents' families?"

"Yeah, a little bit—but I'm still an officer—so they probably share more with you and Lincoln. But look, I actually came to tell you something—and then, if you feel like it, we can talk about Jackson and Strader. Man, I hate to tell you, but your car's tires have all been slashed."

Stephen sat there a moment, trying to take it in. "All of 'em?"

"Yeah."

"Shit!"

"Yeah." James reached over and took Stephen's shoulder. "Sorry to tell you the bad news."

"Do you think it was Strader?"

James opened the palms of his hands. "Can't think of anyone else...unless he got one of the residents to do it. In any case, you're being sent a message." Then, changing tack, Fowler asked, "Do you have breakdown coverage?"

"Um, yeah, my ever-practical parents gave me a Triple-A package for my birthday. But the car can't be towed, so they'll have to change the tires here."

"Hey, Stephen, look man, my cousin runs a tire discount garage not too far from here. How about I call him and see what he can do for you? Why don't you go out and see what size you need?"

Stephen vacantly nodded his assent as he walked out of his office. He decided he would walk past Melvin Strader—without showing any emotion—just to see how Strader reacted.

"Leavin' already, Chaplain?" Melvin was impassive.

"Nope. Just thinking about getting new tires—hell, maybe even a tracked vehicle. What do you think?"

Melvin's eyes blinked like a ventriloquist's dummy. Stephen knew he had called Strader out by what he had said, but he wanted the officer to know he wouldn't be daunted.

"Hey, whatever lights your candle." Melvin dropped his head and tried to look busy with some forms on his desk.

Bullseye, Stephen thought. He knew he and Strader had entered the territory of 'I know that you know that I know.' Now it was a question of who blinked, or got shot, first.

Once Stephen had checked his car's tire size, he went back to his office where James was waiting. When he gave James the tire size, Fowler proceeded to call his cousin. Then it hit Stephen.

"Hey, James, I don't have a checkbook with me and I don't own a credit card."

James lifted a hand for silence. "It's cool, Rev, I have your back. Pay me when you can."

Ten

It was later than usual when Stephen got back to his little cottage. He saw an old pickup truck parked near his landlord's house, but didn't give it much thought. Instead, he was focused on the fact that the lights were on in his place and Emily's car was in the drive. As he switched off the engine, Stephen sat there for a few moments reflecting on how good it made him feel knowing that someone who loved him was waiting inside. He chuckled to himself that he had started to become domesticated. He had never been a particularly 'wild child,' but as one of his seminary professors had said to him, "Travis, you are untamed." And compared to the others in his seminary class, he was—no wife and no desire to be in a safe, middle-class parish. Then he remembered one of his favorite books, *The Little Prince*, wherein the fox teaches the Little Prince about what being tamed means— the joy and anticipation that comes from having someone special in this life. With that, Stephen got out of the car and quickly made for the door. In parody of all of the wholesome television shows he had watched as a kid, he called out, "Honey, I'm home!"

Emily's head appeared around the corner from the kitchen with a cocked eyebrow. "Are you all right?" But it was said with a smile. They both had a good laugh at themselves. "Supper is nearly ready. What kept you today?"

"Let's eat first and then I'll dump the whole load on you."

"That bad, eh?" They kissed.

"Probably worse, but let's eat first. What kind of day did you have?"

"Boring, compared with yours, but I was able to run a lot of lab tests. Inching further toward my degree."

"Ah, my beautiful and brilliant mad scientist!" Stephen helped Emily bring the food to the table.

"Are you sure you're okay?"

"Yeah, I'm okay. The prison system is shit, but I am okay—very okay, because I have you in my life. And I love you."

"Are you trying to get laid?" Emily looked at Stephen with a somewhat furrowed brow, "Because you know, you don't have to try this hard." She winked at him.

"No, that's not it." He took a bite of food and chewed it thoughtfully for a minute. "I have simply realized what a contrast there is between my work and home life. And I am truly thankful for you."

Emily lifted her napkin and wiped her mouth. "Well, thank you. I am thankful for you, too. Please tell me there are no 'buts' to follow all of this effusive praise: 'I love you, but...'"

"Not at all. I do have bad news to share, but it's not about you and me."

"Stephen, please go ahead and tell me what has happened today!"

"If you're sure."

"Yes! Talk!"

The rest of their meal was taken up with Stephen relating the day's events and all of their implications. Emily sat back in her chair. "I can't believe what's going on there!" She let out an exasperated sigh. "Can't you get the police involved?"

"If I want to get fired, I can. But my getting fired won't sort out the crap that's going on at the center."

"Fired? Why?"

"Chain of command. I would be going outside the chain of command. In theory I must first go to Warden Harris and, only after that, should I go to Ralph Martin. But neither of them is going to do anything. Well, to be accurate, Harris would go to Melvin Strader, who would then probably shoot me—like he did Jackson. Or, if I went to Martin, he'd blow me off because of my not taking it to Harris...and either way, I get shot." Stephen laughed sardonically as he shook his head at the predicament. A heavy silence settled over them for a moment, but it was quickly broken by Emily.

"I have an idea. When I am out in the field, mucking about with animals, it's difficult to take notes. So I use a small cassette recorder. What if you took it to meet with Ralph Martin? And, say, put it in your briefcase? That way, if he helps you, all is well; but if he 'blows you off,' as you say, then at least you have evidence that you tried to do something."

"Who would have thought that being a prison chaplain would have felt like being a spy? But I think you're right. There's no way I can talk to Harris about what I know; but if I went to Martin, then at least the 'higher ups' in the correctional system could see that I didn't go outside their beloved chain of command—especially if I have proof."

"Sorry to sound so cynical, but I also think you need to confirm the day the recording will be made."

"How so?"

"Well anybody could—if they wanted to—contest or challenge at what point in the process you spoke with Martin. But if you, for instance, recorded part of the radio news on the morning you meet with him and then recorded what you are about to do, that would help prove when you spoke to him. And from what you've told me this evening, the sooner you meet with Ralph Martin, the better."

"My lover, the sleuth. But I suppose you're right. I had better call Ralph tomorrow and make an appointment. I'll do it after I have spoken with James and Lincoln. They need to know what I am doing—we're all implicated in this now."

"Look, Stephen, in case Martin asks you to come to his office right away, after you call him tomorrow, let me show you how the recorder works. It's in the trunk of my car."

Emily slipped on her shoes and went out to retrieve the cassette recorder. They spent the next hour or so practicing with the sound settings when it was hidden in Stephen's briefcase and then his coat pocket. Once they were satisfied that he had mastered the art of surreptitious recording, they went to bed. Not surprisingly, Stephen's sleep was once more invaded by various personalities in the Jackson affair. It wasn't long before Emily began stroking his brow, trying to calm him as he thrashed about. Stephen awoke with a start.

"You know, Reverend, sleep deprivation can kill you just as well as a bullet. It just takes a little longer. What's it going to take for you to relax?"

"Well, I can think of something," Stephen offered tentatively.

"Am I supposed to guess?"

"It might be more entertaining," grinned Stephen.

"O-kay then...How about washing your car?"

"Nah. It's an inside sort of something."

"We go in the kitchen and bake cookies?"

"Nope. It's closer than that. It...um, involves the anatomy."

"Right. Well, it could be root canal surgery. Shall I get some tools?" Emily started to leave the bed.

"Absolutely not—no pain is involved!"

"Well, gosh, Stephen. I seem to have run out of ideas at twenty past midnight."

"Oh, just pat around the bed. You're sure to find it." And, funnily enough, Emily did. As a result, they both fell deeply into, what the Bard called, "nature's soft nurse."

~ * ~

The next evening saw Stephen, James and Lincoln gathered at the cottage. As the latter two men had families, they elected to meet early and over dinner. Stephen had picked up some pizzas and laid out a selection of drinks. Emily decided to work late at the lab, in order to give them privacy.

"So we're all agreed?" said Stephen. "We hold a pre-Christmas open house at the advancement center?" Lincoln and James gave their assent.

"We're gonna need some sort of 'playbook'," added James. "We got to keep Strader busy. He's the wily one. So we need to have some signals as to when we move nearby him and try to get him into conversations with other staff or visitors. If we all share the task, it shouldn't be too obvious. Let's face it, he's not that bright!" All three men laughed.

"We'll need to have some music playing—that's certain," added Lincoln. "It will help protect our conversations with the families."

"I guess you're bringing your Perry Como collection?" quipped Stephen.

Parker simply cocked his head as he looked at Travis. "Yeah, right, white boy!" Their laughter was a needed tonic for the business at hand.

"Say, Stephen, your lady friend has a head on her shoulders, to come up with that idea of recording your conversation with Ralph Martin," said James. "So why don't we take it a step further?"

"What do you mean?" asked Lincoln.

"Here's what I mean." James leaned closer to his audience of two. "If we got ourselves two more small recorders, we could record all of the conversations we have with families at the open house. If the correctional system doesn't want to do squat about it, we'll have plenty of evidence for the State Bureau of Investigation."

"Hang on a minute, James," interjected Lincoln. "Why would the SBI be interested in a case involving wrong-doing inside the prison system?"

"Well, generally, they wouldn't...but..." Lincoln and Stephen waited. "But they have jurisdiction when there is criminal activity to do with state property." Lincoln started to object, but James simply lifted his hand. "Listen, man, where else can we take it? The pissant police in Fairborn? And we don't yet know whether this car selling to inmates' families is limited to the advancement center or is also going on at other units. A local police force would have to hand it on to the state sooner or later."

"James is right, Linc," Stephen said.

"Yeah, yeah, I can see that now. But should we let somebody in the SBI know what's going down beforehand?"

"Normally, I'd say yes," Fowler spoke up. "We shouldn't even have to be doing this. But, man, after working in this state system for the last eight years..." He shook his head in near despair. "Man, the only people I trust in this system are sitting right in front of me. But look at us. Two black guys and a counter-cultural white padre—sorry, Stephen. Who's anyone gonna believe?"

"No offence taken," responded Stephen, "But you're right. Even in supposedly post-Jim Crow North Carolina there's still too much deeply embedded racism. And hey, I was a conscientious objector during Vietnam. We're not exactly mainstream, are we?"

"No," James continued. "We need to build an air-tight case before we present whatever we find. Stephen has the written documents from those who were willing to share them. Now we just need those recordings and we'll have something to give the SBI—and if we all go there together, they might just get the idea this is too big to cover up."

"And if that fails?" asked Lincoln. "Man, I don't want to be a nay-sayer. But what if the SBI doesn't take up the case?"

"Then I'll send copies of what we have, and copies of the recordings, to every big newspaper on the East coast. This shit's got to stop or we haven't done our jobs."

"Amen, brother," said James.

"Yeah, you're right—unfortunately. Just call me the reluctant third 'Musketeer'!" James and Stephen both looked at Lincoln. "Hey, guys, don't worry. I'm in this thing with you." He held his hand out so the others could join him. "All for one and all of that shit!" They laughed and each seemed to breathe more easily.

At that moment they heard the front door open. Lincoln and James turned quickly to see who it was. "Don't worry guys, it's Emily," explained Stephen.

Emily came through the door and saw three faces look in her direction. "Hope I'm not interrupting?"

Stephen quickly jumped up and went to greet her. "Not at all. We're just about finished. But let me introduce you to James and Lincoln." Both men stood.

"Now I see why Stephen has a spring in his step!" smiled James.

"And you're much nicer to look at," quipped Lincoln. "Did you know your man had a 'hero complex' before you fell for him? Watch out he doesn't involve you in all of this."

"Too late," replied Emily. "But I wouldn't have him any other way."

As James and Lincoln were on their feet, each said his goodbyes, as they wanted to get home to their families. As James stepped out the door, he turned and said, "See you on Thanksgiving."

"Wouldn't miss it," said Stephen. "Anything you want us to bring?"

"Just yourselves—and a good appetite. Diane loves to cook for guests! So don't eat for the next two days!" James winked and closed the door.

~ * ~

Stephen decided it might be politic to stop by the advancement center on the way to Fowler's house for Thanksgiving lunch. As he switched off the engine, he asked Emily, "Would you mind waiting here for a few minutes? I just want to check on a couple of the guys and..."

"And you don't want to have your tires slashed again?" injected Emily.

"Yeah, something like that."

"Don't worry. Just do what you need to do." She patted the dashboard, "I'll take care of this baby."

As Stephen entered the building, Bill Frazier was on the front desk. He was more concerned with the day's football games than with whoever entered the center. All of the admin offices were shut for the holiday. Stephen gave a brief greeting to Frazier and walked to the dayroom area, which opened onto the dining area. A fair number of residents were decorating the dining hall and he could smell the turkey which was cooking in the kitchen. Stephen quickly surveyed the day room to see who was about. A group was gathered in front of the television, also engrossed in the day's games. He caught Marvin Jacobs' eye and nodded toward his office. "Save my seat," said Marvin as he got up to meet with Stephen.

Stephen was surprised to see that Lincoln was in the office. Jacobs went in right after him. "Happy Thanksgiving!" Stephen said to Lincoln. "I thought you would be at home today."

"I could have said the same thing about you," came the reply. "I drew the short straw," explained Parker. As he spoke, Stephen pulled the office door closed and offered Marvin a chair.

Marvin quietly looked at each man. Then Stephen said, "It's cool, Marvin. Linc is up to speed with the whole Strader business." Focusing on Marvin, Stephen asked, "What's the scuttlebutt? Anything new come up? Oh—and any news on who might've slashed the tires on my car?"

"Nah, man, everything just about the same. Nobody's been willing to talk about what happened to your car."

"I figured as much," said Stephen. "Linc and I need to share our idea for trying to get to as many families Strader's hit on as possible." He and Lincoln then explained the idea for an open house before Christmas and what they hoped to gain from it. They let him know that James Fowler was involved as well.

Marvin rubbed his chin and averred, "That might just work. Why're you telling me?"

Lincoln spoke first. "We want you to tell everyone who has been willing to talk about their dealings with Strader about the upcoming open house. They need to be here, if we're going to pull this thing off."

"I understand," responded Jacobs. "When's this thing gonna happen?"

"The second Saturday in December—at suppertime. With all of the eating and drinking and people just generally milling around, we think Officer Fowler, the chaplain and I ought to be able to speak with all the families."

"It make sense," nodded Marvin. "I'll get it done. Anything else?"

"Just this." Stephen handed Marvin his business card with his home number on the back—a clear infraction of the rules. "If anything happens—and I mean anything—with regard to Strader, and I'm not here, call my home number. This is for your eyes only, got it?"

Within seconds, Marvin was tearing the card into pieces, which he then ate!

Both Stephen and Lincoln were taken aback. "What?" came from their mouths at the same time.

"It's cool," Marvin assured them, "I done memorized it. I won't forget." He smiled, pointing at his head.

"Okay, then." Stephen stood to leave. "I'm off for Thanksgiving lunch with the Fowlers. You two enjoy your Thanksgiving."

Stephen was shortly back at the car. "Leave us away," he said with a flourish. He had the directions to James' house written on a piece of paper which he pulled from his shirt pocket and handed it to Emily. "You're the navigator."

Fifteen minutes later, they were pulling up to the Fowlers'. As people usually do when they are told not to bring anything to a gathering, they retrieved a bottle of wine and a floral arrangement from the back seat. Before Stephen could ring the bell, a lanky young boy, perhaps seven years old, opened the door and greeted them. As Emily and Stephen introduced themselves, they noticed a smaller sibling hiding behind her brother. She had lovely corn rows with tiny ribbons at the back. Stephen dropped to one knee and spoke to her as he offered his hand. She tentatively took it in hers and said, in a giggly voice, "You're white!"

Stephen looked with terror at his hands and then yanked up his shirt sleeve. "Oh, my gosh! You're right! I'm white all over! What shall I do?" His diminutive hostess laughed with delight.

James' head popped around a corner and said, "Baby girl, I have already told you about our guests. Don't make a fuss." Looking at Stephen, he winked and said, "Not everybody gets to be black. The Lord God just chose some of us." James then appeared in full and said, "Welcome!" And then, seeing the gifts, he said, "Now I told you not to bring anything! Diane, come out here and see what the good chaplain and his lady friend have brought us—even though I told him not to do it. Don't ever serve in the army, Chaplain, if you can't follow orders." Diane soon joined them, wiping her hands on her apron.

"So good to meet you, Stephen. James has told me so much about you."

As Emily proffered her hand introduced herself, James interjected, "Now this is the woman who's made a changed man out of the chaplain." Stephen felt himself blushing.

"Mmh-hmm, you see?" He pointed at Stephen.

"Well, I see you have met Letitia and James, Jr—but we call him Jimmy," stated Diane. "They're a little excited, because...well, to be honest, which James says I can be with you, none of James' white colleagues has ever been here. I hope you don't mind my saying."

"No, I understand. Even in 1979, North Carolina isn't the most progressive state in the union, is it? James and I work in—well, shall I just say—a very peculiar place. In any case, we're delighted to join you for Thanksgiving." Stephen and Emily removed their coats, which James took from them. They were ushered to the living room, where the television was on. The children rushed to see the closing minutes of the Macy's Thanksgiving Day parade.

Diane then laid down the law. "For the next two hours, that TV is off limits. This is also a football-free zone." James was shaking his head, wearing a broad smile. "We are—all of us Fowlers—going to sit, eat and behave like civilized human beings with our guests." Diane looked at her family. "Do I make myself understood?"

"Yes, ma'am," replied Letitia and Jimmy. She then gave James a look.

"Baby, you outrank me! I'm just following orders." Diane gave James a pretend smack and then kissed him.

"Y'all go on in and take a seat. The food will be out in a jiffy." With that, Diane and James disappeared into the kitchen.

Emily and Stephen sat together on the sofa. It only took a few minutes before the youngsters had joined them. Letitia took an immediate interest in Emily's hair and was soon running her fingers through it. "Your hair's different," remarked Letitia.

"What do you think about it?" asked Emily.

"I don't know," mused Letitia, "It's soft...and kinda fluffy." With that, she took both hands and tossed Emily's locks into the air, giggling all the while.

Diane looked from the kitchen and said, "Baby girl, what are you doing with Miss Emily's hair? She might not want you to do that." Then, turning to Emily, Diane said, "She's not in school yet, so she isn't used to hair other than African-American."

"It's all right, really. I'm enjoying the attention. I'm a scientist, and science is all about curiosity. She can't hurt it anyway."

"Oh, don't be too sure about that," retorted James. "Just don't let her try to give you a haircut!"

In a matter of minutes, James and Diane had placed all of the food on the table. They sat three on each side. Diane had one child on each side of her and Letitia took the seat opposite Emily, her newfound friend. James asked Stephen to ask the blessing over the table laden with true Southern fare: roast turkey with stuffing, candied yams, green beans and mashed potatoes. There was a large pitcher of iced tea to wash it all down. They all joined hands for the blessing, and when Stephen had finished, James stood with aplomb to cut the bird. As he made the first incision, he stopped momentarily and said, "I should let you know that Di has made pecan pie for dessert. So be sure to leave a teensy bit of room!"

Plates were passed around, family style, to be loaded with turkey. James then helped the children with their plates. Stephen and Emily waited for everyone's plate to be filled, but Diane was having none of it. "Y'all better start eating before the gentle giant digs in! Nobody's plate is safe then."

"Can't help it, baby! I've told you what it was like growing up with seven brothers and sisters. Meals were a free-for-all! I never ever got enough to eat—"

Diane cut him off, "Before you joined the army. I know."

"Well, they don't," James winked at Stephen and Emily.

Soon everyone was eating. Even Jimmy and Letitia were momentarily distracted from their guests by the feast before them. Diane talked about her work as a primary school teacher on the outskirts of Raleigh. After a pause, James looked around Stephen at Emily and said, "Stephen hasn't told me nearly enough about you—'cept he gets this dr-ea-my look in his eyes whenever he mentions you." Stephen pretended to stab James' hand with his fork. "Now, Rev, don't get violent, man!" Stephen shoulder-bumped James as they both laughed.

"I do research on things which affect herd animals—cattle, sheep, goats and the like."

Jimmy piped up, "What about turkeys?" Letitia giggled.

"Good question, Jimmy. But I tend to work with four-legged creatures."

Before she could continue, Letitia joined in, "What about fish?"

Emily made a false-frown and squinted at Letitia, "Now young lady, when was the last time you saw a herd of fish walking around on four legs?" More giggles. Diane gave her children that look which signaled 'enough.' The signal was received.

"I'm doing my doctoral research on environmental effects on animal health. Air and water pollution, contaminants in food, etc. I spend about half my time on farms and the other half in the lab, running tests."

James nudged Stephen, "This woman's a keeper—and she's about as far from prison work as you could get."

"Amen to that," added Diane. "But that's as much as we're talking about prison today." James lifted his hands in surrender. "I keep hoping James will find something else—anything else. But listen to me going on—already breaking my own rule!" With an abrupt change of tack, she asked "How long have you two known each other?"

Both Emily and Stephen started to speak, so he deferred to her. "About six months now. We met when we were out riding bikes early last summer."

"That sounds about right," interjected James. "That's when our chaplain started kicking up his heels."

"Oh, James, leave him alone," Diane reached across the table and gave him another playful slap on the hand.

Stephen simply chuckled in a good-natured way. "Falling in love will do that to you." He squeezed Emily's hand under the table.

The banter of four adults getting to know one another continued in that vein through dessert, until the two children could sit still no longer. "I wanna go outside," said Jimmy. "Some of the guys want to play football this afternoon."

"What do you say?" asked his mother.

In an exaggerated way, Jimmy said, "May I please leave the table?"

"You may," answered his father, adding, "You too, baby girl. But don't y'all go farther than the Robinsons' house. Understand?"

Both children replied, "Yes sir," and then made a dash as though their parents might have a change of heart.

Once the little ones were outside, Diane spoke first and said, "I'm going to break my rule for just one minute." Looking steadily at Stephen, she said, "I know what you, James and Lincoln are planning to do at the open house. And I support it, but after what happened to that Jackson fellow—and not to mention getting your car's tires slashed, Stephen—I want y'all to be very careful. James hasn't been in harm's way like this since he got home from Vietnam. There's nothing about your jobs that's worth losing your lives over. Just don't y'all try to be heroes. And as for you, James, the children and I need you in one piece—so just be aware of when you need to cut your losses. I'm sure the same goes for Emily."

"Well...yes, I agree their lives are important; but I have to confess that I came up with the idea of recording conversations— if only to prove that neither James nor Stephen had anything to do with pressuring inmates' families to buy worthless cars. I want this thing to end safely too."

They sat with their thoughts for a few minutes. James looked at Stephen and asked if he would say a prayer for them all. "Certainly," he replied. The four of them joined hands around the table. "Creator God, you have made humanity in your image, yet so often it's difficult for us to recognize your image in others—because of our bad choices and actions. Help us to fight the good fight, and not to fight with anger or bitterness, but only with your love, justice and righteousness. We pray that no other lives be lost for the sake of human greed. In Christ's name, Amen."

Following the prayer, Stephen turned to Emily and said, "I think it's time we left these two in peace."

"Which will only last until the children come home," quipped Diane. They all stood. "Stephen, thank you for your prayer. I'm so glad finally to have met you—and your lovely girlfriend. Let's do this again."

James fetched their coats. As they hugged their hosts, Emily and Stephen thanked them for the feast. The late autumn sky was now darkening, so as the guests left, James went out to call in Jimmy and Letitia. He gave Stephen and Emily a wave as they departed. James looked at the clouds which were forming ominously in the west and felt a slight shiver—not of cold, but of dread.

Eleven

On the Monday following Thanksgiving, Stephen arranged an appointment with the Director of Chaplaincy Services, Ralph Martin. It was for that same afternoon. During the morning, he went by Katz's office to let him know that, as Martin hadn't responded to the copies of the car bills of sale which Travis had sent, he wanted to see Martin's reaction when he presented himself that afternoon.

There were butterflies in his stomach as he entered the chaplaincy office suite in this grey cathedral of corrections. As usual, the blue haze from cigarette smoke marked the way into Martin's office. Stephen reached into his jacket pocket, felt for the 'on' button and pressed it. Show time, he thought.

Peggy smiled when she saw Stephen, "Well, hey, stranger! Haven't seen you for a while."

"Good to see you too, Peggy. Whew," Stephen waved his arms at the smoke. "You must have asbestos lungs to live in this environment."

Ever cheerful, she said, "Oh, I get used to it. Chaplain Martin is expecting you, so go right on in." Stephen's eyes began to burn as he followed the smoke signals.

"Good afternoon, Stephen," began Ralph, "What brings you here today?" Martin actually seemed somewhat cheerful. Stephen wondered whether he dared to hope.

"Did you have a good Thanksgiving?" Stephen thought it best to begin with chit-chat.

"Oh, not bad—well, until I watched the Oilers and Bears play."

"What happened? I was in a football-free zone."

"Oh, it wasn't so much a game as a travesty. The Chicago Bears were brutalized by Houston, thirty to zip. Anyway, have a seat. I'm guessing you didn't come here to ask about football scores, did you?" Martin fired up a cigarette and started fiddling with it nervously.

"No, I didn't." Stephen opened his briefcase and pulled out the documents. Ralph, as you are aware, I have even more bills of sale to families of residents at the advancement center. But there's more..." Martin's face had already hardened into a frown. He drew heavily on his cigarette and cocked an eye at Stephen, as he held the cigarette between his teeth. Stephen was trying to give as much information as possible before Martin could break in and stop him.

"Are you aware that Walter Jackson—who disappeared from the center—died of a gunshot wound? As you will recall, there were gunshots at the center the same night Jackson fled. If you'll just look at these bills of sale, you'll see the name of Officer Strader's brother, Vance." Stephen stood and placed the papers on his boss's desk. Martin's jaw was trembling, but what happened next surprised Martin himself. He suddenly clamped his teeth so hard that he bit through his cigarette, which fell into his lap. He stood up in a fury, swearing and brushing at his clothing. "Goddamnit, Travis! What are you trying to do to Officer Strader? Do you want his job?"

"His job? W...what do you mean? I have no interest in being a security officer."

"No. I mean do you want him fired? Is that what you want? Who do you think you are? Some self-ordained security policeman? Don't you think he has his own chain of command? And haven't I told you to use your chain of command?"

Frustrated, Stephen butted in, "But we report to the same man, Ralph; and he's useless! That's why I came to you the first time! The residents at the center—and their families—are suffering due to Strader's shenanigans and Harris's inefficiency! Their well-being *is* my concern!" Both men were shouting. Only then did Martin notice that his office door was open. He took a deep breath, got up, clearly trying to gain control of himself, and closed the door. Martin could only snort, as he was still clamping his jaws, his face an almost mauve color. Stephen wondered if the man was about to have a stroke or heart attack.

Then, in an avuncular and clearly patronizing tone, he asked, "Stephen, by what authority do you work in this state's correctional system?"

"I'm not sure what you mean. Apart from having been hired by you, I assume I'm here under the same authority as you—Jesus Christ, the Lord and Head of the Church."

Sitting back down, Ralph went on a rambling exposition on the calling to ministry, eventually arriving back at the whys and wherefores of prison ministry. Travis was lost in the word-spill. Then Martin reached into his jacket pocket and produced his lighter. "I'm destroying all of these documents, just like I did with the ones you sent me. You've got no business with them! You stick to your role." Martin lit them one by one and dropped them into the waste bin.

Stephen had to bite his tongue when he nearly mentioned that they were only copies. Looking satisfied, Martin looked up at Stephen, who was still on his feet, and said, "Now git back to your job! And don't forget to close the door behind you."

Stephen picked up his briefcase and opened the door. Peggy's face was slightly paler than when he had entered. Stephen wondered whether this might be the last time he would be in this office. Peggy never looked up from her typewriter as he passed. Stephen wondered whether—if it came to a trial—Peggy would be asked to testify. She had obviously heard everything.

~ * ~

"Good Lord!" was all Emily could say after Stephen played back the tape. "Is the man crazy?"

"I don't know," replied Stephen in a completely flat tone. "Ben Katz thinks he's manic-depressive. So, yeah, maybe he's mentally ill." Stephen had lifted his arms in questioning mode but let them flop lifelessly on the dining table.

"Is there anything I can do?" Emily reached across the small table and took his arm.

"Go for a walk with me? The rain has stopped and I need some fresh air."

"Yeah, you smelled like an ashtray when you got home!"

"Thanks."

"No, I didn't mean it that way; it's not your fault!"

"Yeah, sorry." They put on their coats and stepped out into the late November air. Stephen took several deeps breaths. "I felt suffocated enough from Martin's smoking—*but his attitude!* 'By what authority are you working in the prisons?'" Stephen mimicked Ralph's voice. "I'm so frigging tired of everything prison! The staff are as bad as the inmates—sometimes worse!"

"Do you think Martin is somehow involved with Strader? He seems keen to protect him—or at least keep you off his case."

"I don't know. There are over a hundred prisons in this state. Why would he get so involved in one?"

"Maybe it's a scheme which is in more than one prison?"

"I've thought about that too. It's certainly possible. But we won't know until we get more information and convince the SBI to investigate. They have the skill and resources to deal with this."

Stephen hesitated and then added, "They're also armed."

"Do you really think it's that dangerous?" asked Emily.

"Well, Jackson's dead and someone slashed my car tires—that's certainly a warning. Lincoln thinks I ought to buy a gun."

"Seriously?"

"Yeah, seriously. Can you imagine me a gun-toting minister? What sort of gun do you think Jesus would have carried? I can see me in a gun store: 'Have you got the Apostolic Automatic?' And the extra-large Matthew Magazine?"

Emily gave Stephen a loving punch. "I don't like the idea either. I guess we'll have to be extra careful."

"You're right. I can't help but believe that if Mr. Jesus were alive today, he would tell his followers that 'those who live by the gun shall die by the gun.'"

They walked in silence for a few minutes and then Emily asked, "Do you think Ralph Martin could be jealous of you?"

"Where'd that come from? Why would he be jealous of me?"

"Well, you say he's a depressive, that he chain-smokes, and he's divorced—how old is he?"

"I've never asked, but from what he's told me about his life, I'd say he's in his early to mid-fifties. Why do you ask?"

"Strictly on a superficial level—and as a woman. If I had a choice between a young, fit, good-natured and healthy man and a middle-aged, depressive, ill-humored man—there'd be no contest.

It's just a thought. And then maybe he's simply burnt-out—and doesn't want you or anyone to create more work for him? I don't know. But what I do know is this: As a minister, you are doing what is ethically right, not to mention what is legally right. Why the hell isn't your boss supporting you?"

"Perhaps we'll find out once the investigation takes its course—which won't be soon enough for me. I'm really getting fed up with it all."

~ * ~

A week or so after Thanksgiving, Stephen noticed a new young man in the day room. He was pasty-white, with baby pink skin. His face seemed to be in a permanent sneer. As Stephen entered the office, he quietly asked Lincoln about the new arrival. "Kinda young to be in here, isn't he? He's certainly no long-timer."

"Who, the butthead?" asked Lincoln without looking up from his typewriter.

"He's got a nickname already?"

Parker stopped his typing. "Just from me. I had to help process him here." Lincoln had the new guy's prison 'jacket' or file on the desk. He flipped it open with disgust. "Elton Bohannon Matthews, III—there's a name for you! Twenty-one years old."

"Is he why you're pissed off?"

"You're damned right! It pisses me off when we have guys coming through here who did nothing more than steal a television and got put away for twenty years and then some privileged white kid comes here with a rap sheet as long as his arm. Listen to this!" Travis took his seat. "He steals a car in Raleigh with a friend, over Thanksgiving break from college. They drive it to Myrtle Beach. On the way they stop in a town and smash the plate glass display window of a motorcycle dealer, and steal a motorcycle, which our young Mr. Matthews rides while his buddy drives the car. On the way to the beach, the bike runs out of gas, so he torches it. Then, when they arrive in Myrtle Beach they rob a couple of their cash at knife point so they can have spending money. And as if that wasn't enough, when they drive the car back to Raleigh, they torch the car. Some good citizen saw them as they set the car alight and called the police." Lincoln caught his breath and leaned back in his chair. "So, what've we got here?" He started enumerating on his fingers. "Grand theft auto, malicious destruction of property, breaking and entering, motorcycle theft—and destruction—armed robbery and then more destruction of property. And what does his daddy do? Arrange with his golfing buddy judge to reduce it all to a fucking misdemeanor!"

"I can see why you're steamed. He obviously got the best justice that money can buy."

"And while I helped process the kid's paperwork, he sat there with a smirk on his face, as though it were all a joke to him—which I'm sure it is. Hopefully the other residents who've done real time, will help make his stay as unpleasant as possible." Stephen chuckled unintentionally at an intrusive thought.

"You think this is funny, Rev?" shot Lincoln.

"No, not at all. I was just remembering an incident that happened up at the women's prison a few years back—how the inmates sorted out a particularly nasty woman."

"Do tell."

"The inmates gave her a chunky whirl."

"A what?" Lincoln was puzzled.

"You've been in the correctional system two years or so, and you haven't learned about this inmate-to-inmate punishment?"

"I'm listening," said an intrigued Parker.

"Well, you take your average toilet bowl, fill it with human excrement, three or four people grab the victim and stick her head

109

in the toilet bowl and flush. *Et voilà*, zee chunky whirl." Stephen made a flourish with his hand.

"Damn! That's just plain nasty!" exclaimed Lincoln, as he experienced an involuntary shudder—but he laughed all the same.

"Yeah, well, it worked."

Lincoln paused thoughtfully for a moment. "You know, Stephen, the longer you work in this system, the more you find yourself laughing at things people on the outside wouldn't necessarily find funny."

"Amen to that."

"And who would've thought we'd have to be more cautious around the staff than with the inmates?"

"The public have no idea. Did you ever hear about the prostitution ring my chaplain supervisor ran with the trustees at the women's prison?"

"Just a bit—it happened the year before I started working here."

"Well suffice it to say, he wound up behind bars—but in a Federal open prison." Stephen shook his head as he recalled the situation. "He was white, of course, so no real time to speak off. But at least he was defrocked."

Changing the subject, Stephen asked, "Linc, have you bought your tape recorder yet?"

"Yes, I have. Marcella's been practicing with me. It should be cool."

"Roll on open house! This crap is taking up too much of my waking time. Let's just hope we get the goods. And we each need to make a backup copy—just in case."

"Out of curiosity," enquired Lincoln, "Where are you keeping the paperwork?"

"Well, let's just say it's under lock and key."

"Well, look man, don't you think it would be a good idea to let me and James know where the evidence is?" And then added, "Just in case—as you said?"

"Sorry, man. You're right. You know Benjamin Katz—staff psychologist up the hill?" Travis looked in the direction of the women's prison. Lincoln nodded. "Well, if anything happens to me—just ask Ben."

The two men then turned their attention to planning the open house that was only a week away. They had decided that the families of the residents would each bring a dish or snack, as they had too small a budget to cover their planned soiree. It would consist of finger food, so that Fowler, Parker and Travis could move easily among the families.

"And the day after the open house, let's meet at my place to play through the recordings," offered Stephen. "Oh—I haven't told James yet—I am going to speak with my brother-in-law, Dave, in Winston-Salem. He's a trial lawyer and we can trust him. I just want to find out where we stand legally with what we're doing— and get any advice we might need."

"You afraid we're all gonna wind up cellmates?" laughed Lincoln.

"Hell, Linc, who knows? We just can't take anything for granted. I'll let you and James know what Dave says. He can probably help us make the case."

"Man, it still blows my mind how nobody in the correctional system wants to make a link between the gunshots on the night of Jackson's disappearance and him winding up dead of a gunshot wound."

"Yeah, I know," agreed Stephen.

"Look, Rev, have you done anything about what I suggested—getting yourself some protection?" Lincoln mimicked a gun.

"To tell the truth, no. I just can't bring myself to do it."

"Just watch your back then. Hey, I gotta get back to this paperwork, if you don't mind."

"Nah, go ahead, there's something I need to do." Stephen left and went straight to weights storage in the exercise yard. There was one resident bench-pressing and another spotting for him. They both acknowledged the chaplain and went back to the task at hand. Stephen picked up a two-and-a-half-pound weight and sidled over to one of the picnic tables. He sat on the table top for a few minutes and then left his signal for Marvin Jacobs. He then thought about his car—he had meant to park down the road from the center. He decided to swing through the parking lot to make certain his car hadn't been attacked again. Stephen remained immobile for a moment, trying to decide whether or not to move his car. He fiddled with his keys in his pocket—but then something caught his eye. Something was stuck under the driver's side windshield wiper. Lifting the wiper, something rolled loose: a bullet. A chill ran down Stephen's spine and he instinctively looked all around him. He fished a handkerchief out of his jacket pocket and picked it up. It was a .38 caliber. He hurried back into the office and showed his find to Lincoln.

"It was on your car?" Lincoln whistled softly. "Man, that's a clear threat if ever I saw one. What are you going to do with it?"

"Ideally, I'd like to have it dusted for prints, but I don't know if I should do it now or once we have all the evidence we can gather."

"Talk with Fowler—he'll be in at second shift today. I'd do whatever he suggests. But, damn Stephen, you'd better be careful—extremely careful!"

"After the tire business, I had intended to park down the road a way. But I forgot. Have you or James had any weird shit like this?"

"No. But I reckon one of Strader's stooges knows you're the man holding the hard evidence. Whoever it is, I'm sure his family has been sold a car by our friendly Strader brothers. And I'm relatively certain he's being threatened with being sent back to finish out his sentence. But since Jackson's death...well, as you can imagine, not many guys are willing to say much."

~ * ~

"A bullet on your windshield?" James was incredulous. He rubbed his head, shaking it back and forth. "Man, oh man!! They have your number."

"So what should I do?"

"You didn't touch it, did you?" asked Fowler.

"Only with my handkerchief." James gave an approving nod at Stephen's response.

"I've got a cousin in the police—but he's over in Greenville. Still, that might be better, as it's not too close to where this shit's going down. Let me take it and I'll get it to him—" James broke off as a new thought came to him. "What caliber bullet killed Jackson?"

"I have no idea."

"Well, Stephen, just you get yourself in touch with his widow and see if she can get the police report. If the bullet didn't pass through him, it will be in the forensic report."

"I'll call her this evening on my home phone. I'm not feeling too comfortable about using the office phone."

"You're right about that. From now on, you, Linc and I will only speak about this face-to-face or from home."

There was a tap on the door. Stephen excused himself from James and went to see who was there. Delbert Moore was waiting, with a sheaf of papers in his hand. "Hey, Chaplain, may I bother you?" He looked past Stephen and saw Officer Fowler. "But not if you're busy. I can come back."

113

At that, James stood and said, "We were winding up anyway. Come on in, Delbert. I've kept a seat warm for you." To Stephen he added, "Catch you later."

Holding up the papers in his hand, Moore said to Travis, "I could use your help again. It's another paper."

"Yeah, sure. When do you need it back?"

"No later than Thursday, if possible."

"Great. Thanks." Neither man said anything, but it was clear Delbert had more he wanted to say.

Stephen felt the pun seeking escape, "Anything more, Moore?"

"That was bad!" exclaimed Delbert, but he chuckled nevertheless. "But yeah, there is more. I'm hearing things...disturbing things."

"Such as?"

"Such as it's becoming common knowledge that you're helping several residents with their Strader problem. Although nearly everybody is on your side, many are saying you're going to get hurt; that you can't take a hint. You don't have to be a hero, you know. I mean, look at me. I tried to fight the corruption in our county sheriff's department and I'm the one serving time."

Before Stephen could respond, Delbert was re-living what had got him locked up: The sheriff's dirty dealings, the mole on the town council, the planting of evidence at Delbert's home, the kangaroo court and the injustice of it all. Stephen almost had the urge to say, "Stop! We've covered all of this before—many times!" But, of course, he didn't. That is not what chaplains do. What they do is operate as a bleed valve for the frustrations of the incarcerated who are cut off from their worlds—from friends, family, lawyers and others. Before Stephen knew it, an hour had passed, but realized he was only hearing 'yada-yada.' He worried that his eyes had glazed over or that Delbert knew he wasn't paying attention. As he re-focused, he recognized that Moore was on auto-pilot rehearsing all he had said before. Stephen felt he had dodged a bullet—but then the word 'bullet' shifted his thinking back to the threat left on his car's windshield. He sneaked a peek at his watch. It was already five-thirty and he was getting hungry. Finally, he interrupted Delbert's flowing narrative. "Delbert, I'm really sorry, but I need to leave soon."

Realizing he had come to pass on a cautionary warning to Stephen, but had erupted in self-pity, Delbert apologized. "I'm sorry, Chaplain. I really hadn't meant to blab on and on about my situation. Just be careful, okay?"

"I'll do my best. Oh—Delbert? Will you have any family coming for Saturday's open house?"

"Yeah, I hope so. I'm guessing you'll be there?"

"I had better be. Lincoln and I planned the whole thing! See you then, if not before."

"Okay, and sorry about taking so much time."

"That's what I'm here for."

~ * ~

On his way home after work, Stephen decided to take a different route—just in case. He realized the entire day had gone by and he hadn't spoken with Emily. As he turned down the lane that led to his cottage, Stephen noticed an old pickup truck parked on the other side of the road about one-hundred yards from his home. Was it the one he had seen before? Stephen realized how paranoid he was becoming, but then he chided himself—was it paranoia or realism? A man was dead and Stephen had received two clear threats from...someone. Should he double back and get the license number? He decided against it, switched off the engine and went inside. The first thing he did was call Emily's lab at the university. Happily, she picked up the receiver. "Hi, lovely. Good to hear your voice."

"Where are you—at work?" she enquired.

"No, just got in. Crazy day—but I'll tell you about it in person. I need to make a call right now—to Jackson's widow. More weird shit is happening."

"Your voice sounds tense. Are you okay?"

"Yes and no. Shall we stay at your place tonight?"

"Sure—any particular reason?"

"Not sure."

"Stephen, you're being enigmatic. Are you sure you're all right?"

"In a general sort of way...yes, I'm all right. I'll be better for seeing you. I'll drive over in about thirty minutes, okay? I love you."

"Love you too—but I'm still concerned about you. See you soon."

After Stephen had hung up, he fished in his briefcase for the piece of paper with Thelma Jackson's number on it. He dialed and waited. A world-weary voice answered. "Mrs. Jackson? This is Chaplain Travis."

"Oh. Hello."

"Do you have a few minutes to speak with me? I believe it is important."

"Well, all right."

"Mrs. Jackson, did you ever receive a police report concerning your husband Walter's death? It should have been with the coroner's report."

There was a brief pause. "I don't rightly remember. But I think my brother has all of that. Perhaps you could give him a call?"

"I'll do that, Mrs. Jackson. I'm sorry to have bothered you."

"That's all right, honey, I'm just glad someone is interested in what happened to my dear Walter. Goodbye."

Travis then dialed Roy's number. It rang several times when, to his surprise, an answerphone kicked in. After the recording, Stephen left a short message. "Roy, this is Chaplain Travis—we met at Walter's funeral. Could you by chance tell me what caliber bullet killed Walter? It's urgent." Travis left his number before hanging up and then wondered—too late—if that had been a good idea. Time would tell, but he felt there was wasn't much time left.

Stephen gathered a few things, along with his briefcase, and went out to his car. It was dark, but he thought he could make out the pickup in the shadows. He reversed out of his driveway and turned away from the truck. As he rounded the corner, he saw lights behind him. The lights remained behind him—at a distance—until he pulled along the curb outside Emily's house. The truck pulled in about one hundred yards back. Stephen was torn between walking up to the driver and going inside, so he lingered on the sidewalk, all the while staring at the truck. What if it were Melvin Strader? What if he were armed? His musings were broken by Emily's voice.

"Are you ever coming in? Supper's ready."

"Yeah, yeah, here I come." Stephen mounted the steps and kissed Emily. "I think I might have been followed. In fact, I'm sure I was followed." Stephen stood just out of sight alongside one of the large sash windows and peered up the street.

"You're not joking, are you?" In that same moment, the pickup pulled away from the curb and drove slowly past the house.

Stephen pointed at it and said, "It was parked outside my house. It followed me all the way here. Now whoever it is knows where you live as well."

"Y'all gonna eat?" came Charles' voice from the kitchen. "We're waiting for Stephen to say grace." Charles was only half

117

joking. All the roommates had grown up in the church. And as they were scientists, Stephen was their only live clergy-specimen to observe and study.

"C'mon." Emily took him by the hand. "Let's eat and then talk." Stephen simply nodded and followed her.

Charles made a histrionic effort of folding his hands and bowing his head. "Asshole," said Stephen. Charles gave an equally histrionic wide-mouth show of being shocked, after which Stephen intoned *haMotzi*.

Pat said, "I like that Hebrew blessing. It kinda makes it special. Thanks."

"You're welcome." As he sat, Stephen said, "I just realized I never ate lunch today. I'm famished!"

It was another one of Charles' pasta specials: Chicken parmigiana. Ever the extravert, Charles looked at Stephen and said, "You don't look yourself. Can you share it with your friends?"

Stephen hovered between barking out, "Mind you own business!" and welcoming the opportunity to unburden himself. He chose the latter.

"You'd better have time to listen. This is going to take a while." All three of his companions looked at him—even Pat— although she gave him the owl-blinks first. Stephen began with the night Jackson disappeared and brought them to the present day, with its 'bullet warning' and being followed to their house.

Soon the three scientists were all chipping in their ideas for solving the questions. Charles and Pat congratulated their housemate over her idea of tape-recording conversations. Charles went one further and suggested they all buy some cheap instamatic cameras and take photos of anything out of the ordinary—especially the pickup truck. Emily said she would buy the cameras tomorrow. Then she added, "You know, if I were studying a disease among cattle, I would first try to identify whether the problem was bacterial or viral. Viruses are a lot cleverer than bacteria—and it's harder to knock them out. So then, Stephen, is this guy Melvin Strader a bacterium or a virus?"

"I would say he's a bacterium. He's wily, but he's not bright. After all, if it were indeed he who fired those shots at Jackson, that was an action born of desperation. And once we get the police report on the bullet that killed Jackson, we'll be a step closer to identifying the gun's owner...well, provided it's registered or has been used in a crime before."

"Stephen? Do you actually think this Melvin guy, or his brother, might shoot you?" Charles asked earnestly.

"I have to assume so. I mean, there's only one way to find out if he's bluffing, right? And I'm not thrilled with the idea."

"Maybe you should stay over here more often?" replied Charles. "He wouldn't shoot all of us, would he? And there would be more of us to keep an eye on you and on whomever might be hanging around."

"That's a kind thought, Charles. And it's worth thinking about. But my fear is to put any or all of you into danger because of me and my work. It doesn't seem fair, or right."

"Let's put it to a vote then," said Charles. "Who is for letting Stephen stay here as often as he needs to?" Three hands shot upwards. "There, that's settled then. Try not to spend time alone at your house."

"Thank you," said Stephen. "I'm truly touched—I just hope you've taken on board how dangerous this might be. It's no small thing."

"Hell's bells," piped up Charles, "I've been beaten up more than once for being queer. What's a little gunplay? This is the South, after all."

Stephen and the others laughed despite the gravity of the situation. Pat interjected, "And I was bullied at school for being...well, just for being." She turned her owl's gaze toward each person at the table.

Stephen actually felt moved to tears. He reached for his handkerchief and then remembered he had left it with James Fowler when he had handed him the bullet. He picked up the napkin from his lap and wiped away the incipient tears. "Sorry, guys. I hadn't realized how emotional all this was becoming for me. Thanks for your support."

Emily placed her arm around him and leaned her head against Stephen's. "We're not just disembodied brains, you know. Sometimes we scientists actually care about people."

"Okay, thanks. Message received. But I'll expect you all to be as forthright if you find this situation becomes too much for you. Hopefully, things might change after this weekend—once the open house has come and gone."

Twelve

"Dave? This is Stephen." Travis held the receiver between his right ear and shoulder as he fished the pen out of his pocket. "Have you got a few minutes? It's business."

Dave Andrews was married to Stephen's sister, Ella, and ran his own legal practice in Winston-Salem. "Where are you? In town?"

"No, I'm not in town, I'm still in Raleigh, but I need to pick your brains about how state laws and due process work for inmates. We've got...well, a bit of a situation here between the inmates and staff that is certainly against prison regulations, if not in contravention of state law." Stephen doodled a bit while he listened, in order to get the ballpoint working.

"You remember, don't you, that one of the papers I wrote for the *Law Review* was about what sort of minimum due process is afforded to prisoners? I'm all ears."

"Yeah, I thought this might interest you." Stephen set out

for Dave all of the happenings from the beginning until the present.

"Damn! So a prisoner has died, shots were loosed on state property and no one has investigated it?"

"That's about the size of it. But don't forget some of the shite I told you about that happened at the women's prison. These correctional system hijinks aren't that unusual—but they are insidious. Corrections is a different world. It has its own rules—they just don't seem to be the ones written in the handbooks. But look—please don't bother telling my sister about any of this, okay? She'd just get worried and then say something to our parents, and I don't need them worrying and asking about it."

"Well, you're a minister and I'm a lawyer," quipped Dave, "So we're both bound by confidentiality, eh?"

Stephen laughed, "Yes, I guess we have it covered."

"So here's the deal. You say that inmates—or residents—at your facility are having their families pressured into buying clapped out cars by one of the guards and/or his brother. Right?" Stephen assented. "Is any of the money changing hands on the prison grounds?"

"I have reason to believe it is—and certainly the men whose families are involved have the bills of sale here. But, of course, they all bear the name of Strader's brother, Vance."

"Hmm," mused Dave, "Although inmates in North Carolina's prison—or any state prisons for that matter—are legally denied certain Constitutional rights, like those covered by the Fourth Amendment—"

"Hang on! Remind me what that covers."

"The Fourth Amendment covers things like search and seizure—of drugs or the like—and also warrantless searches. So when one of the prisons has a major search...what do y'all call it?"

"A shakedown," replied Stephen.

"Right, when a prison has a shakedown, they do not need to have a warrant to search the cells. And, of course, the guards can take anything that is deemed by the prison to be contraband. So in those instances, certain rights don't obtain. Still with me?" checked Dave.

"Yes, so far."

"Okay. But let's say that during a shakedown a guard used excessive force on an inmate to get him or her out of a cell. Any injury to that inmate would qualify for due process under state and federal law. Remember, the state sends people to prison *as* punishment, not *for* punishment. And there's a big difference embodied in those prepositions. The incarceration, being removed from society, is the punishment; inmates should not be any more liable to bodily injury or harm than anyone in free society. Clear?"

"Understood." Stephen was scribbling note on a pad.

"So, the same applies to inmates if their families are being coerced into financial dealings—particularly with the staff. So help me understand why that hasn't happened."

"Where do I start? As I mentioned, we follow a chain of command—not unlike what you experienced in the Air Force. If you go outside of that chain—even as a chaplain—you're subject to reprimand. It's up to the individual above you in the chain to decide whether or not you went outside the chain for a good reason. But even with actual bills of sale in my hand, it wasn't a good enough reason for the chaplaincy director to initiate an investigation."

"Think he's in on it somehow?"

"You're not the first person to ask that. But I have no idea. In any case, where do we go with this—the SBI?"

Dave thought for a moment. "As you're in Raleigh, why not go straight to the top?"

"What? The governor?"

"No. The attorney general's office. He'll know who to put on the case. And if your colleagues go with you, there's less of a chance that it will be swept under the carpet. Do you have copies of everything?"

"Absolutely. And we'll do the same with the sound recordings."

"Great. If it's not too much trouble, send me copies for safekeeping." And then Dave added those troubling words, "Just in case."

"Christ—you're about the third person to say that to me! I'm starting to get paranoid!"

"Sorry, Stephen. But you did say one person is dead already, and that your tires have been slashed—and then there's the bullet on your car. I don't mean to worry you, but if something—anything—should happen to you, I'll be on it. You're more of a brother to me than brother-in-law. I'll fight your corner."

"Thanks, I mean it, but I am worried. Lincoln, the social worker with whom I share an office, thinks I should get a gun. But that's so much against my principles. I'd rather quit the job than think I had to go around protecting myself from my co-workers!"

"But you won't will you—quit I mean. It's not in you. And, unless you are prepared to shoot or kill someone, don't carry a gun. The other guy would shoot you first—so don't give him a reason."

"I'll try not to make myself a target. Hey, I've got to get back to the center. I called you from home because it's hard to talk confidentially at the unit. Thanks for your help."

"Stay safe."

Stephen put on his coat and picked up his car keys. As he glanced around the room for his briefcase, his telephone rang. He thought it might be Dave calling him back. But the voice at the end of the line was both gentle and countrified. "Rever'nd Travis?" Stephen acknowledged the caller, not yet recognizing the voice. "This is Roy McNair—Walter Jackson's brother-in-law?"

"Yes, of course! How are you?"

"Fair to middlin', fair to middlin'. You asked me for some information and I wanted you to know I got it."

Stephen didn't want to sound over-excited, so he breathed deeply before replying. "I hope it wasn't too much trouble."

"No sir, it warn't no trouble. But to answer your question, the bullet they dug out of Walter was a .38 caliber." Stephen could feel his heart pounding. Could Strader be that stupid or that cocky, to use the same size bullet as a threat?

"Rever'nd?"

"Yes, I'm here—I was just thinking. Thank you, Roy! I really do think this is going to help find Walter's killer. May I ask one more favor?"

"I'll do what I can," came the reply.

"Do you have the original forensic report or a copy?"

"Oh, they give me a copy. Why is that?"

"Would you mind if I used it? Could you send it to me or I could come and get it from you?"

"Just give me your address and I'll have it to you directly. It ain't a problem."

Stephen gave Roy his address and checked his watch—he was late for work. But then his brain and conscience told him: this *is* your work.

"Rever'nd? You want to know what the pity of it is?"

"Yes, please."

"You know, poor ol' Walter didn't die from the gunshot itself...the poor soul bled out, I guess while tryin' to get home."

~ * ~

When Stephen arrived at his office, James Fowler was on the front desk. As Stephen greeted him, James silently mouthed, "I have news" and looked down the corridor in the direction of Stephen's office. Stephen simply nodded and kept moving. Lincoln was in, so Stephen knew he could share what he had learned from Dave Andrews. But before he could say anything, Parker spoke first.

"Marvin Jacobs says you want to see him. Oh—and Fowler says he wants to see both of us. He's got some news."

Stephen responded, "Let me catch Marvin first, and if there's any news. I'll fill you and James in at the same time." Stephen went to the day room and, not seeing Marvin, took a look in the dormitory area. Jacobs was lying on his bunk, reading a magazine. Stephen called his name.

"Hey, Rev, I got your message. Why don't we take a walk to your office?"

Both men joined Lincoln and, as they sat, Marvin looked Stephen over and said, "Whassup, Rev? You're looking a little concerned."

"That I am," responded Stephen. "Tomorrow's Saturday, and that means the open house. What are you hearing from the guys whose families bought cars from Strader? How many are coming? And do you know if they're willing to talk?"

Before Marvin could reply, Stephen spoke again. "I would also like to know if you have any idea who's been using my car as a message board?"

"Whoa, Rev. Calm down. Let's take 'em one at a time, bro! Everyone who's been involved with Strader and his brother has been told to get they families here. They know it's important. But you know there's that old sayin' about leadin' a horse to water. I 'spect you'll get maybe five families. But that oughta do. The rest

126

of these guys, well, they just tryin' to get by and get out. You can't blame 'em."

"No, I guess you're right."

"As for who's been sending you messages...I got an idea, but I ain't sure yet. Gimme a few more days. That all?" Jacobs stood to leave.

"Yeah, thanks, Marvin."

As Marvin opened the door, James Fowler was just about to knock. "Officer Fowler! Come right on in!" Jacobs bowed in clownish fashion as he made way for James, who pulled back his fist in pretense of a punch which wouldn't follow. "I'm going, I'm going," chuckled Marvin.

Fowler quickly looked over his shoulder—something all three men were beginning to do with frightening regularity. He closed the door behind him and said, "My cousin called me last night. They lifted clear thumb and index finger prints from the .38. And they got a match. Seems it's someone known to the justice system. And more specifically, he's currently serving time—" James paused for maximum effect, "right here in the Fairborn Advancement Center for Men."

"Damn, brother, spit it out!" exclaimed Lincoln.

"It's our own Tyrone Mason."

At first Stephen was speechless. Then he blurted out, "Holy shit! I trusted that guy! He knows so much of what we're doing!" He leapt to his feet and began pacing.

Lincoln was slumped in his chair, rolling his head back and forth and saying, "Man, oh man, oh man!"

Running his hand through his shaggy locks, Stephen was talking more to himself than his colleagues. "What the fuck?! What's Tyrone playing at? And what about tomorrow night?"

Fowler laid his strong and steady hand on Stephen's shoulder, and gave him a light shake. "Hey, man, it's gonna be all right. It might not help, but Tyrone's family has been leaned on by the Straders as well. I don't know if the man is playing both sides against the middle or hedging his bets on who's gonna win this battle. Look, brothers, has Tyrone actually lied to any of us? Think about it."

Travis stopped pacing and Parker sat forward in his chair, both in deep thought. "No," averred Travis, "In fact, he underscored my doubts about Harris—and he asked whether I knew who actually was running the advancement center. Maybe that was a hint...I don't know."

Fowler turned to Parker and asked, "What kind of time does Tyrone have left on his sentence?"

"I think about six years," Lincoln replied. "Why?"

"It's just a lot of time to face when a man's so nearly out of the joint. I'm guessing he's given us as much honesty as he dares while giving Strader what information he needs to stay off Tyrone's back. See what I mean?"

Both men agreed with Fowler, although they were still in a state of shock.

James continued, "I mean, after tomorrow night, what's it gonna matter anyway? We'll have our recordings and the paperwork. If that doesn't spark an investigation, nothing will!"

Stephen wasn't sure. "But if Strader knows we'll be talking to the residents' families—what then? He'll be watching us like a hawk."

"Maybe," countered Fowler, "But there are three of us and only one of him. And even if he knows what we're up to, he'll also know we'll be watching him."

"What about Tyrone Mason?" asked Lincoln. "He'll be there as well."

"Yeah, well, just leave Mr. Mason to me," James smiled. "He and I are going to have a little chat about his fingerprints." He winked at the two younger men. "Oh, and I got us a meeting at the attorney general's office for the Tuesday following the open house. That should give us time for making copies of everything."

"How come none of this seems to faze you?" asked Lincoln.

"Because, young bro, I saw a lot worse than this in Vietnam. We're gonna do this thing. Besides, we have a holy man on our side, right Rev?"

"Believe me, I've been praying about this!" Then he remembered his conversation with Roy McNair. "My God! I nearly forgot to tell you that I spoke with Walter's brother-in-law this morning. The bullet that killed Walter? It was a thirty-eight."

Thirteen

"You're sure you want to come?" Stephen was pulling on his coat.

"What girl wouldn't be thrilled by an invitation to a prison soirée? It's so romantic! Besides, you said families of staff were welcome, didn't you? And I happen to be your significant other. Anyway, what can happen tonight?"

"You could be positively identified with me—that's one thing. You could become a target for the brothers Strader, for another. That's what worries me most."

"You forget, Chaplain, that this woman has done time. I'm willing to take that risk—for you." She kissed him and said, "And you wouldn't want the residents and guests to miss out on all the chocolate brownies I've made, would you? And you know, after tonight there should be plenty enough evidence to hand this over to the state authorities. You can let it go."

"Let's truly hope so. Have you got your camera?"

"Yes, I've told you. It's in my handbag."

"I've got the tape recorder in my sport jacket," Stephen mumbled to himself.

"Sweetheart, try not to be so nervous. You're going to be fine." And then, in a parody of her own Southern accent, Emily added, "Don't yew let that redneck sombitch rattle yew, honey-chile!

Stephen guffawed. "Thanks, I needed that! Well, let's go."

They walked out into the brisk mid-December air. Once Emily was seated, Stephen handed her the tray of brownies. Before getting into the car, Stephen took a good look around—no mysterious pickup truck as far as he could see.

"Brrr!" shivered Emily, "Let's get this thing going. It's cold!"

Stephen turned on the ignition and reversed up the driveway. They listened to tapes of Christmas music on the drive to the center. Stephen said it would help put him in a festive mood—or as festive as possible, with what lay ahead.

When they arrived in Fairborn, the parking lot was already half-full. Stephen walked around the car and took the brownies from Emily, so she could get out. He quickly scanned the cars in the fading light. With no one in sight, the two produced their cameras and started taking pictures of the license plates of any car Stephen couldn't recognize. Then, there it was. The same '67 Ford Fairlane that he had seen on the night of the shooting. He mentioned it to Emily as he took a picture. They pocketed their evidence and headed for the front door.

When they got inside, Lincoln was dressed as black Santa and acting as MC for the evening. His jolly greetings to the guests replaced the 'ho-ho-ho's' with 'yo-yo-yo's! He seemed to be relaxed and enjoying himself. The renditions of traditional Christmas songs, as performed by various Motown groups, were blaring from the cafeteria, courtesy of Lincoln. Black Santa approached the newcomers and produced two candy canes. "Yo-yo-yo...damn bro! You call that a Christmas outfit? You're dressed just like you are every day of the week!" Turning to Emily, Lincoln took her outstretched hand and kissed it. "At least you make my white brother look good! Hang tight a minute, 'cause I want to introduce you to Ms. Santa." Parker looked amongst the gathering throng and called, "Paging Ms. Santa! Marcella Claus, where are you?"

An attractive young woman with a medium length afro and a pronounced baby bump approached them. She wore earrings of tinsel and a Rudolph sweater. "You called, Santa dear?"

"Marcella, it's time you met my office mate, our chaplain, Stephen Travis and his lady friend, Emily, um... Emily—?"

"Webster." She took Marcella's outstretched hand, followed by Stephen.

"I've heard a lot about the two of you." Stephen indicated the bump.

Marcella patted her belly and sighed, "At least it's going to be a winter baby. I couldn't bear to be this big in the summer!"

"Hopefully the baby will be a nice Christmas present," said Stephen.

"It better not! It's not due until mid-January!" Then, dropping her voice, Marcella leaned close to Stephen and Emily and said, "My Christmas present would be to have Lincoln out of here! And you know what I mean." She rolled her eyes upwards and lifted her hand, "Please, Lord!"

"I'll add it to my prayer list," said Stephen. Then seeing that Emily still had the tray of brownies, he said, "Let me take those." As he passed by Lincoln, he whispered, "Wired for sound, bro?"

"You better believe it," came Parker's reply. "It's showtime!"

Stephen took the brownies to the tables where the food was laid out. Noticing a bowl of fruit punch, he poured two cups for himself and Emily. Then he saw James Fowler in conversation with some family members of a resident. He waited until he could catch Fowler's eye and when he did, James signaled for him to come over. James introduced him to the family and then excused himself for pulling away for a moment.

Trying to look nonchalant, James whispered to Stephen, "Melvin's brother is here."

Unsure of whether he had heard Fowler correctly, Travis queried, "What?"

"Vance Strader is here. Don't look yet, but he's in the corner by the kitchen door. You won't miss him because he looks like Melvin. So we have two of them to keep tabs on."

"Three" added Stephen, "If we count Tyrone." James nodded and his eyes searched the room.

Then Stephen remembered the Ford Fairlane. "James, do you know what car Vance came in? Because there's a car out there that was here the night Jackson split."

"What car is it?"

"You can't miss it. It's a revved up '67 Fairlane—light blue."

"Let me have a peek out there and then later I'll ask who drives it."

"Good luck," said Stephen, "I'd better start mixing."

He took the punch to Emily, "Let's meet some of the folks, shall we?" He reached into his jacket pocket and turned on the recorder.

They began mingling among the residents and their families. One or two made an opening for Stephen, by broaching the subject. Stephen offered a silent prayer of thanksgiving. But then forthcoming witnesses dried up, and he became unsure of whom to approach. It occurred to him that he, James and Lincoln had never arranged among themselves to share out the residents' families. Putting his arm around Emily, he leaned in close and whispered, "What if we're all speaking with the same people? We never thought to divide them among us!"

Casually, Emily shook her hair back and said in a normal tone, "Why don't we ask Santa?" Stephen looked around for black Santa, which didn't prove to be difficult. They sidled up to Lincoln.

"Um, Linc? We don't know who's speaking to which families. Who've you seen?"

In between 'yo-yo-yo's', Lincoln pretended to be telling Stephen a joke. "After I give you the names, Rev, throw your head back and laugh like it's the funniest damn thing you've ever heard." He then whispered the names of two families and Stephen did the same.

He guffawed and punched Santa on the arm. "That's good Santa! I'll have to remember that!" About that time, Melvin Strader appeared.

"What's so funny? Why don't you share it?" Strader's smile looked more like a grimace.

Stephen's heart leapt, as he found himself lost for words. Happily, Lincoln coolly filled the silence. "Nah, man, it's a racist joke." He slapped Strader on the shoulder. "I wouldn't want to offend you."

"Racist, huh? Well you told the chaplain—he's white."

Ever so smoothly, Lincoln replied, "Yeah, well I didn't say *what race* the joke was about, did I? Oops, we have some more guests arriving. Stephen and Emily, help me show them where to put the food." Parker took Travis and Emily each by the elbow and guided them away from Melvin.

"Thanks, man. I was worried there."

"No problem. And anyway, you ministers aren't supposed to lie, are you? Let's help these newcomers and then you cool down a bit with your lovely lady. I'll check with Fowler to see what families he's covered and get back to you. We've got it under control."

Emily asked, "The guy who just came over and asked about the joke, was that who I think it was?"

"He's the one. And his brother is here as well. That's him in the corner by the kitchen door."

Marvin Jacobs came along the corridor with his family. He saw Stephen and made a beeline. "Hey, Rev, good to see you, my man! Let me introduce you to my wife, Mary, and our children." The "children" were two strapping young men. One was a senior in high school and the other a freshman at Shaw University in Raleigh. Stephen greeted them all and then introduced Emily. "Unh-huh," responded Marvin, upon meeting Emily. "Now I see why the Rev doesn't stay here late in the evenings no more!" Stephen blushed. "Ha, look at that, Mary! The Rev's done lovestruck!"

Mary slapped Marvin on the arm, "Leave the pastor alone, Marvin!" Turning to Emily and Stephen, she said, "Marvin can't let nobody be—even after all these years." She shook her head and then added, "Y'all are a fine lookin' couple. Don't let Marvin give you no mess!"

"Marvin's okay in my book," said Stephen. "He's a good man. I know you'll be glad when he's home with you."

"Our boys were no bigger than this," Mary held her hand a few feet off the floor, "when Marvin got sentenced." She looked at her husband. "Fifteen long years..." Then she looked Stephen in the eye and said, "And we hopin' it won't be no longer."

Checking around him, Stephen leaned his head near Mary's, "It won't, if I can help it."

Mary hugged Stephen and Emily, and then she, Marvin and their sons went to enjoy the food on offer. Lincoln swooped in on Emily and Stephen and let them know there were only two families that had not been approached. Fowler was going to try to keep Melvin Strader busy for the next little while, that way Lincoln and Stephen could each talk with the last of Strader's car buying scam. But before Stephen and Emily could move to the next victim of the Straders, Vance was standing right in front of Stephen.

"I don't think we've met. You're the chaplain, ain't ya?" Strader put out his hand. Stephen took it in a perfunctory manner, but did not bother introducing Emily. "According to Melvin, you're still kinda new here, still learning how things work."

"Going on nine months in this unit," Stephen replied tersely, as he waited for Vance to continue. Stephen stealthily switched on the tape recorder.

"Melvin tells me you have some funny ideas." Strader's face was heavily pock-marked, and his teeth were stained from chewing tobacco. The breath emanating from his mouth made Stephen want to retch.

"That's interesting, because Melvin and I rarely speak about my ideas."

"Well, Melvin said to me—not so long ago—he said you don't value free enterprise. Ain't that funny, seeing as how you're working here with men who just wanna git themselves jobs an' make some money an' git on with life? A man has a right to earn some money, ain't he? We all gotta live, right?"

"It's the American way," Stephen said in a noncommittal way.

"Melvin wonders if you ain't some kind of socialist or sum'thin'. Now why would he tell me such a thing about a man of the cloth?" Still the hard grimace of a smile.

"I would say that Melvin's the one with funny ideas—and from what you're saying, he seems to spend far too much time worrying about me." Stephen was beginning to feel his anger rising, but stared coolly at Vance, leaving him to do the work.

"Well, my brother Melvin is a real thoughtful guy. He just wants you to fit in and stay safe."

Stephen nodded as though taking in Vance's words. Then he took a risk. "That's a fine-looking machine you drove here tonight. Looks like you've put a lot of care into it."

Vance was caught completely off guard. "My car?"

"Yeah, the Fairlane."

"Um, yeah, it gets me there and back." While Vance was trying to catch up with what had just happened, Emily stepped forward, and looking only at Stephen.

"Isn't it time we had some food? I know I'm hungry." Then half-turning toward Vance, she added, "I'm sure you'll excuse us."

"Make sure you look after your fella. I'll see you later."

Stephen could feel Strader's eyes on his back as he walked away. He whispered to Emily, "Rescued again! Thanks, love!"

"That guy gave me the creeps." Emily fought the urge to look over her shoulder. She didn't want to give Vance the satisfaction of having rattled them both. They picked up paper plates and began to load them with food. "And he wasn't too subtle in letting you know he's on to you. I'll be glad when you three turn over your evidence to the attorney general's office."

"You and me both." They ate without speaking for a while. Wiping his mouth, Stephen said, "Hey, when this thing is over, let's go away for a while—some place where I can forget about this prison crap."

"You're on. Where shall we go?"

"Somewhere far from here. Let's plan something after James, Linc and I turn in our evidence. It can be our Christmas present to each other." Stephen looked around for the last family he wanted to talk to—the Branscombs—and saw that neither

Melvin nor Vance was in their vicinity. "Ready for one more statement from a family?"

"Sure! Let's do it." They dropped their empty plates in a waste bin and Stephen gave a little wave to Ed Branscomb, who nodded that they were ready.

~ * ~

By 7 p.m., most of the families had left and the residents were cleaning up, with the help of Stephen, James and Lincoln. Parker had agreed to make copies of their cassettes, so after a quick reconnoiter, James and Stephen dropped their cassettes into Santa's huge pockets. Marcella came over and put her arm around Lincoln. Patting her bump with the free hand, she said, "Darling Santa? Ms. Santa and her passenger need some rest—my poor legs are killing me!"

James was on duty for the evening, so he urged Parker and Travis to get home with their partners. "See you two on Monday— unless you're leading the worship here tomorrow, Stephen?"

"I'm actually preaching at the women's prison tomorrow, but you know how to reach me if you need to be in touch before Monday."

Before the two couples left, James asked, "Did you notice something odd about this evening?"

"Yeah," replied Parker, "Warden Harris didn't come."

"Right," James nodded thoughtfully. "Instead we get Melvin's evil brother. I wonder whether our good warden was told not to be here?" With that, Fowler looked at the two brothers who were deep in conversation in a corner of the dining room. "Well, never mind. We all got what we came for. Have a good evening. And see you Monday."

The two couples donned their overcoats and walked out into the crisp evening. They said their goodbyes again in the parking lot, and as Marcella and Lincoln got onto their car, Stephen noticed an old pickup truck at the far end of the lot. He started to reach for his camera to photograph the license plate, but there was just enough light from the street lamp to silhouette a figure in the driver's seat. Stephen thought better of it and they got into his car. He took a deep breath and exhaled slowly, "We're nearing the finish line."

Emily replied, "Let's go home and have a glass of wine. We both need to unwind."

"Amen to that." As Stephen put the car in reverse, he checked in the rearview mirror to see if the pickup moved. As he pulled onto the main road, he saw headlights appear from the driveway behind him.

As it was a Saturday night, Stephen wanted to avoid the beltway around Raleigh, which could be like the Roman chariot race in the film *Ben Hur*. He turned onto a state road which ran through one of the few rural areas south of Raleigh; it was both more direct and had less traffic. As Stephen turned, he noticed that the headlights behind him had vanished. He felt the muscles in his neck and shoulders relax. To try to lighten his own mood, he asked, "So what was it like being back in prison—or at least the advancement center?"

Emily gave a snort. "Any prison you can walk in and out of isn't a prison. But talking with the residents and their families reminded me of how normal everyone is. I mean, the only real difference between the average inmate and the rest of society is that the ones serving time got caught!—like I did."

"Getting caught is one thing," said Stephen, "but getting sentenced is another—especially if you're black and/or poor. One thing I know is that justice is a commodity to be purchased by the highest bidder. One of the guys in the unit served eighteen years for stealing a television! Eighteen years! And he wasn't armed when he did it! But he was black. All he had done was steal a

Sears jump suit off a store worker's washing line, use it to wander into the unloading dock at Sears and make off with a TV. Where's the justice in that? The TV was worth maybe two hundred bucks. But it costs the taxpayers twenty-four thousand dollars a year to keep him locked up. That's getting on for nearly a half-million dollars over eighteen years! For one inmate! So it doesn't even make economic sense. But what his sentence does do is to send a clear message to blacks: Jim Crow is still alive."

"Despite my having spent time in prison, I don't think I could do your job—or even Lincoln's. As a scientist I need things to make sense. If an experiment goes haywire, it's my job to research it until I can understand where things went wrong. But knowing that things are wrong, and then ignoring them...that would drive me crazy. And I don't want that to happen to you. It's clear how these last few months have been slowly grinding you down. That's one reason I jumped at your idea of going away—once this thing is in the attorney general's hands."

"Sometimes the 'justice,' such as it is, has to be doled out in prison. Take for example that rich kid I told you about, Elton Bohannon Matthews the third. He commits a shopping list of crimes and is sentenced to an open prison. Once the other residents got wind of his easy time, they went about making his life as miserable as possible, without being caught and given infractions."

"What happened to him?"

"Oh, they short-sheeted his bunk; put his hand in a warm bucket of water—he obliged them by wetting the bed; they replaced his shoes with an exact match, except they were a full size too small. Then came the critters in the bed—such as a black snake. Oh, some jokester placed a dead fish in the kid's locker, in his pile of undies and shirts."

Emily chuckled at the pranks. "Has he tried to get transferred?"

"Maybe, I don't know. But if he has any sense, he'll stick around, because he won't find easier time elsewhere in the correctional system. Meanwhile it continues, because he won't be released until the spring."

Suddenly the inside of Stephen's car was illuminated. "What the heck?" Stephen was blinded by the reflection in his rearview mirror. Whoever was behind him had his full beams on—and the car was getting closer. "Where the hell did he come from?" Stephen asked out loud. He dipped the rearview mirror so as not to be blinded on this rural road. He knew they were approaching a narrow bridge over a river which fed a reservoir. At that moment, the windshield cracked into hundreds of pieces, and then, due to the speed of the car, imploded on both Emily and Stephen. It was then that Stephen realized that someone was shooting at them. "Get down!" he hollered to Emily. She bent down as far forward as she could, while he began to swerve the car back and forth between the edges of the road. The cold wintry air blasting in his face brought him into hyper-awareness. *We must get to the bridge before he does.* Stephen pressed down the accelerator, trying to put distance between them and their pursuer, but with no success. He was amazed at the random thought which came to him in the midst of such terror. *So much for driving an eleven-year-old car.* That thought was dispelled by the disintegration of the rearview mirror. Stephen couldn't control the impulse to look over his right shoulder. When he did, the driver behind took the opportunity to edge alongside him. It was the Fairlane. With heart racing and palms sweating, Stephen did the only thing that was left to do. The bridge was no more than two-hundred yards ahead, so Stephen turned the wheel hard left. As metal crunched and tires squealed, Stephen glimpsed the gun hand still aimed at him. But because the shooter had only one hand on the wheel, the maneuver worked. Stephen succeeded in pushing the attacker's car onto the verge and into line with the bridge's superstructure and abutment. And then blackness.

Fourteen

"Please, won't you sit down?" The attorney general is just finishing a phone call. James, Lincoln and Emily took their seats. "I'm Gladys Evans, Mr. Collins' personal assistant.

"May I offer you something to drink?" Evans looked at each of them. Emily and Lincoln asked for water, but James simply said, "No ma'am." When Gladys returned with two waters, she ventured to say, "If you don't mind my saying, today's paper was full of the story about what has been happening at the Fairborn Advancement Center. That's why you're seeing the AG himself and not an assistant. I'm so sorry for what happened to your chaplain. It almost beggars belief what has been going on there."

"Ms. Webster, here," James indicated Emily, "Well, she and Chaplain Travis have been very close. And she was with him when he was shot. Although he managed to save her life."

Emily managed a weak smile, despite her lacerations and bruises.

"Oh, you poor dear. I admire your bravery for coming here today." In the same instant, Ms. Evans' phone buzzed. She picked up the receiver and then said, "The attorney general is ready to see you now." She stood and opened the door and they entered.

Attorney General William Collins was on his feet to greet the three of them. Before they formally introduced themselves, Collins, stated, "I want you to know that I have cleared my calendar for you today." He gestured toward a clear desk. "We'll be joined momentarily by one of the department's legal team, Karen Stein, who will be leading the investigation." As though on cue, the phone buzzed. He hit the intercom button.

"Karen's here, sir," came Gladys' voice.

"Send her on in. We're ready."

Karen Stein introduced herself first, then Emily, James and Lincoln followed suit, explaining why each of them was here. Lastly, the attorney general shook everyone's hand. As they were seated, he thanked them for having the integrity to bring forward evidence of wrongdoing in the prison system—even to the endangerment of their lives. Then he said, "Let's get started."

James produced the documentation of the car sales between the Strader brothers and the families of inmates. Collins looked each one over and handed them to Stein, who asked, "Are these the originals?"

"Yes, ma'am," replied James. "But we have copies."

"Good," came her businesslike reply.

James, Lincoln and Emily each then helped sketch out the timeline of events over the last three months, up until the night Stephen was shot—who said and did what, how Warden Harris had brushed it all under the carpet and how even Ralph Martin, head of chaplaincy services, had refused to hear out what Stephen had brought to him. "And you need to hear these." James showed them four cassette tapes.

144

"This first one is the last conversation Stephen had with Ralph Martin." He lifted the cassette player from his briefcase and inserted the tape. Collins and Stein noticeably leaned forward on their chairs, as they heard Stephen's voice speaking with Martin's secretary, followed by Martin and Stephen. Emily began to tear up as soon as Stephen's voice was audible. James took her hand and squeezed it. They heard Martin shouting at Stephen and how Stephen had tried to protest his case. Then they heard Stephen being dismissed and the click as the recorder was stopped. The attorney general had his lips pursed and the fingertips of each hand pressed so tightly together, they were turning white.

Lincoln replaced the tape with the next one, saying, "These next three are from this past Saturday night, at the open house at the advancement center. This tape is also Stephen's." Lincoln glanced briefly at Emily, who nodded to him. Collins motioned with his hand to carry on.

Over the next ninety minutes, the five people sat and listened to testimonies from residents of the advancement center and their families, about how Melvin Strader had his brother, Vance, put pressure on them to buy used cars from him. Melvin used the threat of infractions being cooked up at the center or at the residents' places of work in order to have them sent back to prison to finish their sentences if they refused to buy a car. The brothers thought they had the perfect scam—and it worked—until Walter Jackson broke ranks and paid with his life. James reached in his pocket and pulled out a plastic bag with the bullet which had been left on Stephen's car. "Jackson died from a .38 caliber gunshot wound. The same size as this." He laid it on the desk in front of the attorney general, who picked it up and examined it before handing it to Karen Stein.

"Sir?" asked James. "Is it known what size bullet was used on Chaplain Travis?" Emily squeezed his hand.

Collins sat back in his chair for the first time since the recordings were played back. He frowned and rubbed his face—obviously his mind was churning. Ignoring Fowler's question, he looked at his colleague, "Ms. Stein, don't you think that despite our best efforts, we sometimes put the wrong damn people behind bars?!"

"From what we've just read and heard, I couldn't agree more. I'm happy to start my investigation as soon as we're finished here."

"Sir?" James asked again, "the bullet that was used on Stephen Travis?"

"I'm sorry, your question deserves an answer. Which I don't have at present. A gun was found in Vance Strader's car by the highway patrol and it is being processed along with any other evidence as we speak. The shooter, Vance Strader, as you probably have read or heard, was catapulted through the windshield when his car hit a bridge abutment. Happily, he left his gun in the car after his hasty departure."

Karen Stein cocked an eye at Collins. "My apologies," said the attorney general. "The offbeat humor of those of us in law enforcement."

"Don't worry," said James, "It's the same for us in prison work."

Collins opened a drawer in his desk and produced three business cards. "Do not hesitate to call me if you need any further information—or should you remember anything you haven't told Ms. Stein and me today. Karen, could you please also provide these good folks with your contact details, as you will be directly involved on the case."

Karen opened her briefcase and gave James, Emily and Lincoln her card. "Of course, you are all material witnesses, so I will want to keep in touch and interview each of you. But as the attorney general said, please call me if there is anything you think I need to know or if you need anything from me."

Fifteen

Darkness and fog. Impossible to make out shapes or forms. Sounds emanating from under water. Wait. Who's this? A Jewish travelling salesman, named Moishe? He has a suitcase in hand. He's in a city and sees a nightclub touting, "Herschel, the Amazing Jew." Moishe pays the cover charge and goes in. Klieg lights aimed at a stage. A middle-aged Jewish man comes out, unzips his trousers and pulls out his *schmeckle*, which is huge. He proceeds to lay three walnuts on a table. Then he takes hold of his *schmeckle* and 'Whack, whack, whack!' Herschel cracks the walnuts. The crowd is amazed. Twenty years later, a different city, Moishe is schlepping along the streets of Kansas City, when what should he see? A marquee with "Herschel, the Amazing Jew" in lights. Moishe wonders if it's the same Herschel from twenty years ago, so he pays the entrance fee and enters the darkened club. An old man with a walking frame comes out. Once the lights hit him, Moishe sees that it is the same man! Except this time, there are three coconuts on the table. Herschel unzips, releases his mighty *schmeckle* and 'Whack, whack, whack!' he breaks all of the coconuts! Incredible! thinks Moishe. So he runs up to the stage and offers to buy Herschel a drink. They saunter over to the bar, where Moishe orders, and then Moishe tells Herschel, I saw you years ago, I think it was Jersey City, and you broke three walnuts with your *schmeckle*. Now, twenty years on, you've moved to coconuts! That's amazing! What gives? Nu, says Herschel, my eyesight ain't what it used to be. Laughing. Much laughing, Then choking. Pain. Something beeping. But whose laughter? Whose pain? More choking. Like drowning in a desert. Dry. Yet back under water. Coughing. Gasping for air? And then light. Alive and light. Face appearing, kissing lips. Beautiful scent. No Herschel. No Moishe. But Hebrew. *Mah nishmah?* Another face. Bearded man. Rabbi? *Mah nishmah?* he repeats. Then says, "The lengths somebody will go to in order to get a woman to say 'I love you.'" Rain drops on face. Then drops on lips. Salty. Not rain. Tears. Lovely looking woman with tears on face and hair that tickles nose. Tubes on nose. Force eyes to focus. Strange bed. Machines that whirr and beep. Seeing now. Bearded man now smiling. Welcome back!

~ * ~

"Where have I been?" croaked Stephen.

"According to all the films," quipped Ben, "you're supposed to say, 'Where am I?'"

Another kiss for Stephen, while bearded man says he goes to seek a doctor. "Is that Moishe?" asked a befuddled Stephen.

Wiping her eyes, Emily said, "No. And he's not Herschel either. He's Ben Katz—a very good friend of yours. And he's been bombarding you with Jewish jokes, with the certainty that they are better for you than chicken soup! And he seems to have been right—because here you are, awake again!"

148

"Ben...Katz?" Stephen slowly mouthed the name. "Thirsty," he coughed. "What happened to me?"

Beautiful woman now holding Stephen's hand. "You were shot—in the head." Emily choked back her sobs.

"Shot? Where did it happen?"

"At the OK Corral," came a reply. "Where else? See doc, our patient is awake." Ben Katz stepped out of the way.

The neurologist spoke to Stephen. "You had these folks quite worried—and me too, for a while. Pardon me while I shine this light into your eyes. Try not to blink. I'm Dr. Worthington, by the way, your neurologist, and I'm pleased to meet you—finally! Try to keep your eyes open for me."

"Bright," was all Stephen could say. He blinked involuntarily as the light was shone into his eyes.

"That's the idea. Now let me check your vital signs. You won't be aware of it for some time yet, but you are a very fortunate man."

"For-tu-nate..." repeated Stephen. And then, "Thirsty."

"I'll bet you are," smiled Worthington. "I'll call a nurse to bring you some water."

Stephen tried to turn his head to look around the room, but the pain stopped him. Funny bearded man on one side of bed, lovely woman on the other. She was still holding his hand. Nice feeling. A nurse appeared with a cup of ice water, with a straw. "So good to see you awake! How are you feeling?" She raised the back of his bed so he could drink.

"Feel thirsty," gasped Stephen.

"Well, take your time and just sip it. We don't want you to choke." Stephen took several short sips and then nodded that he had had enough.

Dr. Worthington was standing by and watching his patient become oriented to his condition and surroundings. "Stephen, do you think you might feel like answering a few questions?"

"I guess." Stephen looked as though he were awakening within a dream state, unable to distinguish whether he was asleep or conscious.

"Do you know where you are?"

"Um, hospital?"

"Correct. Now, do you know why you're here?"

Stephen looked at the four people standing around his bed. "Not sure," he rasped, "but she—," he stopped and searched Emily's face, with tears streaming down her cheeks. Quizzically, he said, "I love you, don't I?" Emily could only smile through her tears and nod at him. Stephen seemed to look for confirmation from Katz and the medical staff. "Am I married?"

"Are you proposing?" queried Katz. Then to Emily, "Say, 'yes'—I'm a witness!"

Looking back at Emily, Stephen started again, "She..." Stephen squeezed his eyes shut, searching his memory bank. Then he said, "Em-i-ly." Opening his eyes, he looked at her again. "Yes, Emily, we are a family...I think?"

Through her sobs, Emily was able to squeak out, "Yes, we are."

"Um, Emily said I was shot...in the head."

"That's right, Stephen," interjected Dr. Worthington, "Have you any memory of what happened last Saturday night?"

Again, Stephen searched his scrambled brain. His neck, shoulder and torso muscles appeared to go taut as he struggled to remember. Then, with a heavy puff of breath, he sank heavily into the bed, shaking his head in the negative.

"Do you remember the open house at the advancement center?" Emily asked. "Do you remember James and Lincoln?"

Stephen lifted his right hand off the bed and then let it fall as he began to cry. Worthington turned to the nurse and asked for more sedation. Then to Emily and Ben he said, "I think he needs to rest."

"May I stay?" asked Emily, hastily adding, "I won't bother him. I just don't want to leave him."

"Hold on for a minute," replied Worthington, as he conversed with the nurse about sedation by IV for Stephen. Katz was making ready to leave, but the doctor motioned for him to stay.

"Have both of you ten or fifteen minutes to spare?" asked Worthington. "Let's get a coffee or something and go to my office to talk. Scientist that I am, I still feel uncomfortable talking in front of patients—awake or not. The human brain is an amazing organ—and quite a sponge. I have been surprised more than once by what patients who had been comatose told me when they regained consciousness."

Worthington led them to a drinks dispenser. "May I get you anything?" Katz had a tea and the doctor had black coffee. He walked them down the corridor to his office. Worthington motioned them toward two chairs and then perched on his desk.

"Have you any idea of how lucky Stephen is to be alive—not to mention to have regained consciousness? Let me just give you the percentages. Nearly ninety-five percent of gunshot wounds to the head result in fatalities. Your friend is in the five to seven percent who survive—and many of them have permanent mental or physical impairments, or both. Another amazing fact is that he has not needed a ventilator. We're giving him oxygen, of course, but he's continued to breathe normally. It's too early to say for certain, but Rev. Travis might be in the small percent of victims who make a full recovery." The doctor stood and put an x-ray on the screen on his office wall. He pointed to the rear of the cranium. "There's the bullet. According to the police report, the bullet which hit Stephen first went through the door frame. Had it missed the frame; your friend would have died on the spot."

Katz took Emily's hand. She wiped her eyes and nose, and said, "Vance Strader—the shooter—had begun to pull alongside our car, just as we approached a bridge. He had already fired at us at least twice. Stephen made me duck down and then he slammed our car into Strader's. I...I suppose that was at the same moment he fired at Stephen."

"Well," mused the medic, "that maneuver probably saved his life...and yours." Worthington drank some of his coffee and stared into the cup. He then pointed again to the x-ray. "The bullet cracked Stephen's skull, creating about a two-inch divot. I have removed the bone fragments and debris, but the brain is experiencing some swelling—which is to be expected in such cases. There is also a subdural hematoma—or bruising. When I am satisfied that we have the swelling and hematoma under control, I will put in a plate—and then he's all yours. Until then," Worthington finished his coffee in one gulp, "I need to hang onto to him."

Ben Katz stood and walked over to the doctor. Emily noticed there were tears in Ben's eyes. Heretofore he had been stoically brave and cracking jokes. "I'm a weird, brash, New York Jewish psychologist living in North Carolina and working in prison. Stephen Travis is the only real friendship I have developed since coming here. Do your best." He barely looked over his shoulder as he hurried to the door. "Em, I'll bring you some food. Look after Stephen. Let me know if you need anything." Katz disappeared.

As Emily stood to leave, Worthington took her hand. "I'll see that you have whatever you need to keep you comfortable here. I'm sure your presence will help."

Sixteen

"So, Vance Strader is dead?" Stephen visibly sat more upright in his hospital bed.

"Yeah, man, he died just after he shot you," James informed him.

"I suppose there's more than a little poetic justice in that," chuckled Lincoln.

"So remind me of what happened that night," asked Stephen. "I think that part of my brain was shot or cut away!"

"At least you can laugh about it now," threw in Lincoln.

"Well, I can't laugh too hard." Stephen lifted his hand to the bandaged rear of his head. "This incision and wound area is damned sore."

"Well," said James, "Emily was there with you, so she can tell you what happened better than I can." Turning to her, he asked, "You up for a recap?"

"As much as I'll ever be. Stephen, as the neurosurgeon told you, Vance Strader shot you just as you were slamming our car into his. You collapsed over the steering wheel, and our car kept Strader's half-on and half-off the road. As a result, he slammed into the bridge's concrete railing. Because he wasn't wearing a seatbelt, the moment his car hit the bridge, he was flung through the windshield. He landed in the river. I don't know whether he died on impact or whether he drowned...and I can't say I'm bothered either way. He's gone and a lot of people will be much happier as a result."

"Don't sugarcoat it, girl," smiled Lincoln, "tell it like it is!"

"Anyway," continued Emily, "your shot-up and bashed-up car continued on across the bridge and ran off the road into the trees—which is how I got cut and bruised. I didn't even know you were shot until I called out to you and, when you didn't respond, I reached out to you in the dark and felt the blood running down your back."

"So how did I get into hospital? Who helped you?" Stephen was struggling to put the pieces of his life's puzzle together.

"Frankly, I don't remember a lot about it—I suppose I was in shock from all that had just happened. But, I believe it was a pickup truck that stopped along the road where we had run off. A man came down and asked me if we were all right, and I told him, 'far from it'." Emily pulled a frown as she tried to reconstruct the events. "All he said was to look after you and he would go to the nearest phone and call nine-one-one. He never came back, but at least an ambulance arrived, as well as the police."

"A pickup truck?" Stephen repeated. "What did it look like?"

"Heavens, Stephen, I don't know, it was dark and I was shaken up—but it was old—twenty-five or thirty years, I'd say. That's all I know."

"Just like the one that sat outside my house—and yours." Stephen's mind was enlivened by the topic. "And the man, what did he look like?"

"Again, Stephen, I couldn't say. He was white and over sixty—but he had a cap on. It was dark and I was in shock. I'm sorry I can't help you more."

"No, that's all right." Travis was quiet for moment, looking into the middle distance. "And all the while I thought the pickup truck was driven by one of the Straders. Who was it?"

"Did he have wings?" asked Fowler. "'Cause I'm guessing it was your guardian angel. Without him, Stephen, you wouldn't have gotten to the hospital so fast. Maybe you aren't meant to know who it was."

"And the investigation—how's that going?"

"Man, you sound like you're ready to be outta here," said Lincoln. "I don't think they've made a bullet hard enough to break your skull! But Christmas has arrived early at the advancement center! Uncle Tom Harris has been relieved of duty and charged with compounding a felony. Couple of his cracker guards are being investigated as well, but the big news—and I mean BIG—is that Melvin Strader has disappeared." Lincoln paused and then quickly added, "And please don't ask me *where he's gone*, Stephen, because I don't know. I just hope he stays wherever the hell he is. I've actually enjoyed going to work these last few days. Speaking of which, I've got to meet with a couple of residents this afternoon. You leave the center to James and me—you just get better."

Emily gave Lincoln a hug as he left and thanked him for his support. While she was standing, she refilled Stephen's cup of ice water. She smiled at him as she said, "With all of your questioning, I'm sure you'll need this."

Stephen took several long sips. Then he said, "Strader has disappeared? When was he last seen?"

"The last time anybody at the center saw Melvin was the night of the open house," spoke James. "Maybe he sent Vance after you and then decided to run before he could be connected with...um, well, your intended death."

"I just hope the law catches up with him," remarked Stephen. "He deserves a long stretch behind bars." He thought for a few moments and then said, "I guess you two will know what I'm going to ask next. What about Ralph Martin?"

Emily shrugged and looked at Fowler for an answer. "All I know is—and this is secondhand—he's been sent on indefinite leave, while this investigation takes place. He, like Harris, could be facing the charge of compounding a felony. The attorney general's office has heard your taped conversation with him. They know you tried your best. And they know that Martin did nothing about it." Stephen nodded approvingly.

Emily laid her hand on Stephen's brow and stroked his forehead. "Sweetheart, are you sure you want to keep talking about all of this?"

"Believe it or not, it helps. This whole business has consumed so much of my time and emotional energy over the last several months; it just helps knowing that finally some measure of justice is being done."

James stood, saying, "I'm going to leave you two alone." He hugged Emily and said, "You know where I am if there's anything you need. Take care of my man here." He gave Stephen's shoulder a squeeze and stepped into the corridor. Within five seconds he was back, ushering in Dave Andrews.

"Somebody looking for you," chirped James. "Says he's your lawyer." James gave a little wave and departed.

"Dave!? What are you doing here?" Stephen asked.

"Can't a brother-in-law visit his prime client?" smiled Dave, as he walked over to Emily and offered his hand. "I think I can guess who you are."

After introductions were made, Stephen noticed the briefcase in Dave's hand and asked, "You're not here to get me to update my will, are you?"

"That we'll save 'til later. But I do have some papers for you to sign." Dave opened his briefcase on the bed next to Stephen. "Especially as you are suing the state of North Carolina for damages—once you sign in the correct spaces anyway." Dave winked at both Stephen and Emily.

"I am?" asked a perplexed Stephen.

"You bet your ass, you—well we—are. Your lovely Ms. Emily had your colleagues send me copies of the recordings as well as of the bills of sale. And you, my brother, were specifically told to do nothing about felonies being committed in your prison. That is called 'compounding a felony'—punishable by ten years in prison. Not to mention that you nearly paid with your life. It's gonna be damned hard for the attorney general to make a good and reasonable defense for the state's actions—especially as they have set the investigation in motion, two people are now dead, and one has been wounded—my client. In addition, your car's totaled, and we have no idea when you can go back to work."

"Well, the surgeon says—"

"That's all speculation at present." The lawyer in Dave cut Stephen short. "Have you tried working an eight- or ten-hour day yet? No. Do you know you can safely drive? No. Hell, the way things are going, the newspapers are doing a lot of the investigative work for us. And the really good news is—I'm doing this *pro bono*, only covering my costs—but I will let you buy me a case of Chardonnay! And yes, it's my idea to do this—but your sister, my wife," Dave winked at Emily, "thinks you've been royally screwed by the prison system, as do your parents. If I did the normal lawyer thing and scalped you—especially with what's left of your hair, Ella, not to mention your folks, would kill me."

"Love your bedside manner," quipped Stephen, "I guess they taught you that in law school?"

"Yeah, they taught us that after ambulance chasing. Oh, speaking of your parents, have they come down yet?"

"No, I had Emily ask them to wait. I wanted to be able to talk and to look half-normal—particularly so Mom wouldn't fret over me. They're driving down tomorrow. Emily's going to take them the key to the cottage so they can stay there overnight."

"That's good," said Dave. "Now sir, with your permission, could I get you to sign these documents so we can make the state holler over their *criminal* 'criminal justice' system!"

Stephen looked at Emily, "Whatcha think, lovely?"

"I'd say you've earned it."

"Where do I sign?"

Dave produced a pen from his jacket pocket and used the lid of his briefcase for signing. "It's a short hop from here to the office where I am filing this, so I shall leave you in peace. All being well, you'll at least be able to replace that old car of yours!" He leaned over the bed and gave Stephen a hug. "Love you, man."

"You too," smiled Stephen. "Take care."

"You just get yourself well. We still have some mountain hiking we need to do." Dave shook hands with Emily and left.

"Wow, busy day," was all Stephen could muster.

"You're looking tired. Why don't you rest some?"

"Good idea," replied Stephen, "but there's one more thing I need to do first." Stephen gazed at Emily, who returned the gaze quizzically. "I need to ask you if you're willing to marry me. And before you answer, I want to say please don't be influenced by my current condition. Dave's right, we don't know how well I'll be after I'm released from here. I don't want you to feel sorry for me, I just want to—"

"Shut up, please!" interjected Emily. "May I answer what you're trying to ask in such a clumsy way?"

"Yeah, okay."

"I am willing. I've been willing. In fact, I was going to ask you once you were home and we could have some privacy."

"Gosh...really? That's great!"

"Yes, it is, isn't it? Want to get some rest now?" Emily leaned over and kissed Stephen's lips. "You are my home," she whispered. The smile remained on Stephen's face as he slipped into the healing embrace of sleep. Emily smiled over her lover as his breathing slowed into a rhythm of calm and peace.

~ * ~

"Mom, Dad, I want you to meet Emily, my fiancée." Stephen positively beamed as Emily walked around Stephen's bedside to meet his parents. Paul and Doris Travis were prepared for the worst when they had come to visit their youngest child and only son. Doris simply erupted in tears with the cross-current of emotions—tears of joy, surprise, relief, worry. They were the sort of feelings parents have for an injured child, of any age, along with the heady emotions that come when the last child to marry announces such intentions. Stephen watched bemusedly at the emotional tsunami which flooded the room.

Paul Travis, shaking his head, came over and hugged his son. Doris was hanging onto Emily, whom she'd only just met, crying into her shoulder. "Son, you never cease to surprise," said Paul. "Honey, would you let Emily breathe and come speak to your son?"

Dabbing her eyes, Doris apologized to Emily for the outburst, and turned her attention to Stephen. The gauze bandage around his head brought more tears from his mother.

"Mom, it's okay—I'm okay. Really. I'll be going home soon. There doesn't seem to be any lasting damage. I just have a small plate in the back of my head—guaranteed not to rust!" Stephen tried to inject some humor.

"Oh, Stephen, trust you!" Doris bent over and kissed his forehead. "We've read all about the horrid things that happened in your prison—it's just unbelievable. And for a chaplain to be shot..."

"Mom, chaplains and ministers, we're still human. Ordination doesn't come with an exemption from violence or even death. Remember Martin Luther King? Anyway, I'm alive. And thanks to Emily, I have so much more to live for." Stephen took Emily's hand, smiled at her as he said, "I can honestly say I'm glad it was my hard head which took the bullet and not yours."

Still dabbing at her eyes, Doris said, "Well, I just wish no one had been shot. I can't believe you're taking it so well."

"I'm taking it well because I'm alive. One inch could have made all the difference. One inch! But here I am, fully conscious, breathing, speaking—loving." He held Emily's hand against his face. "This wonderful woman has spent almost as much time here in hospital as I have. And she wants to marry me. What's a bullet wound by comparison?"

Emily asked if Stephen's parents wanted to sit down. They thanked her and took the two chairs while she perched on the side of the bed. Stephen let his parents know there was a drinks machine down the corridor if they wanted anything, but they declined. Paul and Doris asked all of the usual questions of a prospective in-law: name, place of origin, job and more. Stephen told about how he and Emily had met and their shared love for cycling. Emily described Stephen's first trip to the farm with her and how she had him collecting bull semen. Paul Travis roared

160

with laughter at the picture Emily described, while Doris kept saying, "Oh my!"

The foursome was interrupted by Stephen's nurse when she came to check his vitals and ask about pain levels. She also checked the incision to make sure it was healing well and without infection. She topped up the water jug on Stephen's table and asked if the others wanted a cup. Emily had her bike bottle with her, but Doris and Paul were happy to wet their throats.

After an hour of getting-to-know-you chit-chat, Stephen interrupted the flow by asking, "Mom, Dad—what plans do you have for Christmas?"

Paul looked at Doris and said, "Ask your mother."

"Well, we hope to have your sister, Ella, and Dave over for lunch. We still don't know whether Barbara and Phil will drive up from Lexington or whether they're going with the children to her parents. Why?"

"Just wondering if you'd mind having three guests."

"I'm assuming you and Emily are two of the three—and the third?"

"Emily's mother, Sarah Webster. She's been on her own for years since Emily's father died. We thought we could make it a Christmas cum engagement do. What do you think? We'll help with the food preparation, drinks and clean-up. We won't leave it all to you, mummsy-wummsy." Stephen winked at his mother.

"And don't you start worrying about the menu, dear," said Paul. "You know all of our children can cook and help out."

"Oh dear, what's wrong with me? Of course, you can come—and your mother, Emily. I'm so discombobulated—what with Stephen's injury, finding out that you two are engaged—my poor brain's on overload."

"Just tell Stephen and me what you'd like us to bring," interjected Emily. "Also, you'll find my mother is a very practical, down-to-earth sort, so please don't fret about her. Oh, I'll be driving Stephen and me, and my mother will come on her own."

"Hey, before I forget, Emily has the key to the cottage. It's all clean and ready for you. There is food in the fridge, as well as coffee, tea, wine—use whatever you want." Emily reached into her handbag and brought out the key, which she gave to Paul.

Stephen then pushed the control button for his bed and put it into a semi-reclined position. "I have to admit, all of this excitement has left me a bit drained. Would you mind if I checked out for a bit and had a snooze?"

"Not at all, son. Your mother and I will take our things over to your place and freshen up. We'll eat out somewhere nearby and come over one last time during the evening visiting hours. Emily, would you care to join us? Maybe you can recommend a place to eat?"

Stephen gave a nod of approval to Emily. "They're basically harmless. It's time you had a break."

"I'd be delighted," answered Emily, "And I'd be happy to take you to a restaurant Stephen and I enjoy. Shall I meet you at Stephen's?"

They agreed to a five-thirty rendezvous and, when they turned to say goodbye to Stephen, he had already fallen asleep.

Seventeen

Christmas for Stephen and Emily was subdued, yet joyful. It was subdued because of the bullet wound, surgery and recovery—not to mention giving evidence in the ongoing investigation into corruption within the correctional system. The joy was manifest for numerous reasons: the fact that Stephen was alive and on the way to full recovery, justice was finally being realized for the residents at the advancement center and their families, and the fact that he and Emily were deeply in love and fully committed to each other.

Stephen's sister, Ella, and his brother-in-law, Dave, brought the Christmas turkey, while Stephen and Emily supplied the wine and champagne. Doris had prepared the vegetables and Paul the dessert—his home-made pecan pie. Emily's mother, Sarah, simply enjoyed meeting her soon-to-be-in-laws. Stephen felt truly relaxed for the first time in months. He reveled in being with and watching those he loved enjoy themselves and find mutual delight in one another. Paul cracked the champagne bottle for a toast to the engagement of Stephen and Emily. As the glasses clinked and the bubbly imbibed, Stephen produced a small box from his pocket. Emily knew what was coming so they shared a twinkle in the eye and a smile.

Stephen held the small box up for all to see. Dave was the first to speak, "It's gotta be an engagement ring!"

"You're partly right," answered Stephen. "He then flipped open the box, which held two rings. Simple gold bands with a Hebrew inscription: *tovim ha shana'im min ha'ekhad.* Stephen explained that it was from Ecclesiastes 4:9, and means "Two are better than one." He handed the rings to Emily who, though she knew they were coming, had not yet seen them.

"Stephen, they're gorgeous!" The rings were then passed around the table, everyone admiring the intricate script.

"These come by way of my psychologist friend, Ben Katz, who works at the women's prison. He has an uncle in Manhattan who's a jeweler, so Ben asked a special favor, and we got them in a week's time—special delivery." Over the chatter, Stephen called everyone to attention. "We have skipped the engagement ring and gone straight for wedding bands, because, well, we don't see the need for a lengthy engagement, especially as we're getting married in a week." The hum of conversations abruptly ceased as the family members absorbed the news. "In fact, we've planned it for New Year's Day, as we thought none of you would be working and might have some free time. And if you do have plans, so be it, we're getting hitched regardless!"

"Where will the service take place, Stephen?" asked Doris.

"At Mrs. Webster's church in Salisbury. She's Methodist, just like us. So after calling her pastor and explaining things to him, well...he was happy to help out a colleague. It's going to be simple. Mom, you heard that word 'simple'? It's a come-as-you-are service—except that you have to bring a dish of food. That's non-negotiable or we don't eat! This is strictly a do-it-ourselves service and luncheon."

Paul Travis started laughing. "Son, as I said to you before, you never cease to surprise!" Turning to his wife, he asked, "Honey, are we doing anything on New Year's?"

"Going to our son's wedding, I guess."

Stephen looked at Dave and Ella. "What about you two?"

Ella responded for them. "We have plans for the evening, but not during the day. I wouldn't miss seeing my younger brother—my only brother—getting married."

"Does that mean I have to go?" asked Dave, putting on a glum face.

"Only if you want to live, darling," smiled Ella, showing her table knife.

"By the way, Stephen, will you have your bandage off by then?" asked Dave.

"Hadn't even thought about it," laughed Stephen. Turning to Emily, he asked, "Does it bother you?"

"Not a bit. The Frankenstein's monster look is a real turn-on."

"Who else are you inviting?" asked Doris.

Emily answered, "My two house-mates, and Stephen's three prison buddies: Ben, James and Lincoln—and their wives and children."

"'Prison buddies'—I like that," chuckled Dave. "Makes you sound like Al Capone or something!"

"Which one's the best man?" asked Paul.

"Good question, Dad. Maybe all three? Is that allowed?" mused Stephen.

"It depends, how many rings are you giving this young lady?" laughed Paul.

"I'll work something out with the guys. The main thing is that you'll all be there."

"Don't forget your other sister! Who's going to let Barbara and Phil know?" asked Stephen's concerned mother.

"Maybe you or Dad? Emily and I are going to be quite busy between now and then."

Dave spoke up, "Have you two planned where you're going on your honeymoon?"

Emily and Stephen looked at one another and shrugged. "'Away' is about all we have planned so far," said Stephen.

Dave continued, "I know you admire me as a man of excellent taste, a fine jurist and modest above all—I am suing the state on your behalf, after all! So would you trust me to arrange something in the mountains for you? And would a week be sufficient?"

Once more Stephen and Emily looked at each other, pleased and mystified at the same time. "We'd be delighted," answered Emily.

~ * ~

Stephen and Emily set off for Raleigh after breakfast the day after Christmas. No sooner had they entered the cottage than the telephone rang. "It's probably Mom, worried about some detail for our wedding."

When he put the receiver to his ear, he heard what sounded like James Fowler's voice, talking to someone in the background. "Hello?"

"Stephen, you're there. Great! I'm at the center with Lincoln. Have you read or seen the news?"

"I've kinda had my mind on other things. Why?"

"Melvin Strader's been found! Well, what's left of him. He was found in a burnt-out pickup off some back road in a clearing. He was a crispy critter, so they could only identify him by his dental records."

In the background Stephen heard Lincoln say, "Now that's what I call justice! That redneck cracker ends up being black!" Neither James nor Stephen could help but laugh.

"And there's more!"

"More?" exclaimed Stephen. "How do you top that?" He motioned to a quizzical Emily to share the receiver so she could hear the news as well.

"That pickup truck was last licensed in 1950! And it was registered to one Walter Jackson!"

"Walter Jackson?" repeated Stephen. "What a turn of events! Who could have imagined it?"

"But that ain't all!" James was bursting with excitement. "He had one bullet to the head, from a pistol that wasn't his. It was a pistol Walter had brought back from World War Two!"

As Stephen looked at Emily in bewilderment, he heard James and Lincoln talking. Next he heard Lincoln's voice. "Sounds like Jackson's ghost has had his revenge, doesn't it? But my brother here is hogging all the good news. Now check this out. The police found an empty bourbon bottle in the truck, so are positing that Melvin knew they were closing in on him and took the coward's way out. The remains of a gas can were found in the cab with him, so they reckon Melvin got boozed up, lit the gas and pulled the trigger! Boom!"

Stephen was lost for words. "I don't know what to say—it's all so incredible. I mean, Walter's ancient truck and his gun?"

James took the receiver from Lincoln. "Stephen? Forget ghosts! Remember I said there was a guardian angel in that pickup truck you kept seeing—and which stopped to help you and Emily that night?"

"You did," replied a still-dazed Stephen.

"Well it seems the Lord has loosed his 'terrible swift sword,' and relieved us of the Strader problem forever!"

"No shit!" came Lincoln's voice. "Ghost or angel, I do not care!"

"Amen," was the only word out of Stephen's mouth. He and Emily simply looked at each other, both trying to take in this almost incredulous news.

"Stephen? You still there, man?"

"Yeah, yeah, Linc, I'm here or actually, we're here. I've been sharing the phone with Emily. Do the police know when Melvin might have killed himself—if that's what happened?"

James came back on the phone to answer. "Melvin's been divorced for some time and he lived alone. But no one who lived near him saw him after the night of the open house. His car was still in his driveway. Maybe your angel took him for a last ride?"

Lincoln piped in, "Rev, you're not going to start investigating his death, now are you?"

"No! Not at all. It just makes me wonder, that's all."

"Well we thought this news ought to make a welcome Christmas, wedding and New Year's present! You two lovebirds can get away without having to look over your shoulders."

"You're right," Stephen replied. "It is a gift not to have to worry about the Straders. Getting shot once is more than enough!" He paused and then said, "Can I ask you guys about one more thing?"

"Go ahead," said Lincoln.

"What about Tyrone? Is the attorney general pressing any charges against him for his involvement with the Straders?"

"They've pretty much viewed his situation as a case of extortion. He was caught between a rock and a hard place. The only thing they could nail him for was slashing your car tires. But you'd have to press charges."

"Nah, forget it. Who knows what we would do if we were in the same situation? After months of worry and tension, it's hard to believe that this nightmare is actually over...I mean, apart from the investigation."

"Now I'm not inviting you to come to the center, you hear? But you ought to see the guys. They're walking on air! We got a temporary warden and two new officers, so the place has a totally different feel about it," said Lincoln.

"I'm really happy for the men. Thanks for telling me about them. It makes it all worthwhile," Stephen spoke pensively. Changing the subject, he asked, "Are you both ready for New Year's?"

"Why? What's happening?" jibed Lincoln.

"Asshole," replied Stephen.

"Now, now, Rev, you oughtn't to be talking like that." In the background Stephen heard James asking what was going on. "I'm just pulling his leg," Lincoln replied to both. "Yeah man, my wife, who is about to pop, and I will be there. Don't worry."

James took the receiver. "Diane, the kids and I are ready and waiting for the big day. I wouldn't miss it. You need us to do anything?"

"In fact, yes. I want you two and Ben Katz to be my best men."

"Three best men? How's that gonna work?" queried James.

"I'll let you know on the way! We'll wing it, and I'm sure it will all be fine."

"We'll see you at the church at ten," said James, "And don't you be late!" Stephen laughed as he put the receiver down. Looking at his bride-to-be, he said, "I need to rest. My brain is spinning with all that we've just heard. Kiss my brain?"

Emily kissed Stephen's forehead and he stretched out on the sofa.

~ * ~

New Year's Eve was spent with Emily's mother. Stephen enjoyed getting to know Sarah Webster and learning things about Emily's youth that parents consider 'cute' and enjoy sharing with an in-law-to-be. They are usually embarrassing to the adult child. Sarah herself was a research writer for the sociology department at the University of North Carolina at Charlotte. Stephen could see where Emily got her researcher's curiosity. In addition, he noticed facial characteristics and mannerisms the two women shared. Certainly Sarah was a fine looking fifty-something. Stephen also learned about Emily's father, whom she had barely known. He had been an army captain who was killed in a training exercise at Fort Bragg. It was following the accident that mother and daughter had moved to Salisbury.

The two lovers packed their suitcases for their as yet unknown destination. All they knew was that they would be in the high country of western North Carolina, so packed accordingly. That job complete, they retired to bed early, both in preparation for the big day ahead and in celebration that they were again able to make love. Pausing to catch their breath, Emily and Stephen laughed like teenagers at the fact that her childhood bed squeaked like a rusty door hinge! They wondered what Mrs. Webster must be thinking in her bedroom next-door—but not enough to refrain. At breakfast the next morning, Emily and Stephen were a bit sheepish, but Sarah smiled at them both, saying, "Don't forget, I was young once!"

~ * ~

At ten o'clock, both families and the few other guests began arriving at the church. The roads were quiet as it was New Year's Day and a crisp, winter's morn at that. Most folk were just waking or eating breakfast. But not the Websters and the Travises. Boxes of food and drink were hurried into the church hall. When the

Fowlers arrived, Jimmy ran over to Emily and Stephen and gave them big hugs. Diane brought a large box of flowers, with small bouquets for Emily and the two mothers, and there were boutonnières for the men. Everyone gravitated to the church's kitchen, where food items went either into the refrigerator or the oven. Charles and Pat arrived with another one of Charles' 'Pasta Caroliner' creations and Pat's cornbread. Charles, upon seeing Stephen, called out, "You know you can still back out and run away with me!" Most of the group burst out laughing, but the wedding couple's parents were somewhat nonplussed.

Doris and Paul brought all of the dishes and cutlery. Sarah, Emily and Stephen brought wine and soft drinks. Ben Katz arrived with Kate McIntyre, the other psychologist at the women's prison. Stephen was surprised—pleasantly. Seeing the look on his face, Ben said, "Nu? I thought I'd bring a date. I just met her, but she said she loves a good wedding." Stephen hurried over and hugged both of them and then introduced Kate to Emily and the gathering throng.

Then entered the boisterous family of Stephen's elder sibling, Barbara, her husband Phil and their two girls, who were around the same age as the Fowlers' children. The kids saw each other and immediately began dashing around together. Once Lincoln and Marcella arrived, bringing desserts, the company was complete—except for the pastor.

The pastor of the church, Randy Bailey, arrived shortly thereafter. As he and Stephen had never met in person, Stephen went over and introduced himself. Randy had a passing acquaintance with Emily as they had met on occasions when she was home visiting her mother. Randy observed, "If you don't mind my saying, this might be the easiest wedding I have ever officiated. For most couples it becomes the most over-planned day of their lives, and when one tiny thing goes wrong, it's all tears and disaster. It's also the least expensive wedding I have ever officiated!"

"Is that a hint?" joked Paul Travis, reaching for his wallet.

"Absolutely not! I admire what Stephen and Emily are doing. The money I see couples spending on their weddings is staggering." Then in a stage whisper, he added, "I also have an inkling what prison chaplains earn!"

"They don't pay him nearly enough for what they've put him through," stated Emily.

Randy looked Stephen over, even peeking at the back of Stephen's head, which had a small bandage on it. The pastor looked at the gathered family and said, "He looks incredible after what happened to him! I know y'all are happy to see him doing so well and to celebrate this day with him and Emily."

Diane was busy pinning the boutonnières on all of the men, including the pastor. She gave the bouquets to James, Lincoln and Ben and assigned each a lady to receive them.

Stephen called a quick huddle for the pastor and the three best men. Then the circle grew to include Emily, Charles and Pat. They resembled some kind of sports team discussing the next play. "That works for me," said Randy Bailey.

Stephen grabbed a glass for one of the tables and tapped it with a spoon, calling everyone to attention. "As there are just over twenty of us, we have decided there will be no formal ushering into the church. Let's simply go in as friends and families. We'll all go to the front of the church and stand in a circle together." Stephen looked for Lincoln's wife, who was great with baby bump. "Marcella, please feel free to sit if you like."

She was quick to respond, "With this passenger I have on board—ain't no position feels comfortable! But thank you anyway."

"I'm so glad to be a bridesmaid with you, Pat," exclaimed Charles in his campest of voices. This time everyone laughed.

Stephen looked around the entire group of friends and family. Then he went through a verbal checklist: "Bride, groom, rings, license, pastor—I think we're ready." Pastor Bailey led the jovial party into the sanctuary.

James read from 1 Corinthians 13, followed by Lincoln, reading from 1 John 4—both with their poignant words on the nature of love. When it came time for the vows, Pat held Emily's bouquet. Ben Katz was the ring-bearer. As he took them from his pocket, he said, "It's the desire of the wedding couple that everyone have a part in helping them tie the knot by passing the rings one to another, while Rev. Bailey gives the blessing." Then he reached over and laid a hand on Stephen's and Emily's shoulders. *"Tovim hashanai'im min ha'ekhad"*—the inscription on the rings. "Two are better than one! *Mazel tov!*" Emily noticed just the slightest glistening of a tear in Ben's eye and Stephen noted that Kate was holding Ben's hand.

The rings made their way around the circle and finally into the hands of the pastor. He then had the couple repeat their vows whilst placing a ring on the other's hand. Randy intoned the final blessing and the group erupted with applause. The joy was palpable. There were hugs, kisses and the occasional mother's tear all round.

Ben Katz was heard to bellow over the hubbub, "Nu? Where's the grub?" With that, everyone departed for the church hall.

~ * ~

Toward the end of the feast, as people served themselves dessert, Dave Andrews stood and asked for attention. As folk turned to listen, he pulled an envelope from his pocket. "Stephen, we know your car is totaled. So, Emily, is your car gassed up?"

173

She nodded. "We all have pitched in to give you this present." He handed the envelope to the couple. Stephen deferred to Emily. When she opened it, her eyes widened, and she placed her hand over her mouth as she gave it to Stephen.

Ever the card, Dave piped up using his best game-show host voice. "That's right, contestants, you newlyweds have won a full week at Asheville's Grove Park Inn, in your own luxury suite. And that's not all! It's full board as well!"

"But you can pay the tips!" quipped Ben. Kate gave him a playful nudge.

Emily and Stephen looked at their loved ones and fought back the tears of joy. Stephen managed to croak, "One thing I have learned in this life is that it's not being unloved that hurts, but being loved so much that it makes one's heart want to burst. Thank you." He and Emily hugged each other.

"I second what Stephen said. Tears are funny things," said Emily, "they come out both for deep sorrow and deep joy. Just know that these wet cheeks are examples of our joy in all of you."

"Daylight is in short supply this time of year," said Dave. "You two need to hit the road." There followed a flurry of hugs, more tears, wisecracks and well-wishes. Emily and Stephen hit the road.

Epilogue

Emily and Stephen arrived back home in the mid-afternoon, he offered to carry her over the threshold but Emily suggested he carry a suitcase instead. The cottage was warm and welcoming. His, and now their, landlord had collected the mail for the past week and placed it on the dining table. As Emily had yet to change her address, all of it fell to Stephen to sort through. Emily put the kettle on to boil water for a pot of tea while Stephen looked through what seemed most important. She then lit the tea candle in the warmer on the table. Looking at Stephen, Emily saw his face suddenly change as he looked at a hand-scrawled envelope. The handwriting reminded him of that of Vance Strader. He tore it open and withdrew a short note. Emily looked over Stephen's shoulder as they read:

Dear Rev Travis,
I guess by now you know Melvin Strader has joined Vance

in death. You are a smart man so you are most likly figgering how Melvin would end up in Walter's truck and with a bullet in the head from Walters gun. I wont lie to you, sir, cause I done it. I done it for Walter and Thelma and for all them others the Strader boys hurt. I saw what Vance done to you and your lady friend that nite and it tore me up inside and I had tole you when you come to see us the day of the funeral that I would protect you. I know it don't make it right. And I know you seen me several times outside your house and following you. Im sorry if it scaret you, but now you know why I done it. Maybe you dont want to know this and maybe it aint fair to tell you but I did not want to tell Thelma and it seemed right to tell you being a minister and all. I will accept whatever you deem right to do and only hope that God will forgive me.

Yours truly,
Roy McNair

Emily had to sit after reading the letter. They remained silent, looking from one another to the letter and back. It was Emily who broke the silence. "What will you do with the letter?"

Stephan touched the corner of the paper to the tea candle. "What letter?"

Meet Jack N. Lawson

Jack Lawson grew up in North Carolina. As an ordained minister he worked as a prison chaplain in North Carolina and Ohio. He later served as a parish minister in the US and the United Kingdom. After earning a PhD in Hebrew Bible, he taught both ministerial candidates and lay people in the English counties of Kent and Norfolk. After leaving parish ministry in 1997, Jack worked for The Rural Community Council in Kent, focusing on rural economic regeneration and managing a European Social Fund grant between Kent and Nord-Pas-de-Calais. In the process he developed an intense love of France and the French people. Later, Jack spent more than 12 years as training and development officer for the Methodist Church in East Anglia.

His book, *The Concept of Fate in Ancient Mesopotamia* (Harrasowitz, Wiesbaden), is an exploration of early human attempts at working out how much free will we human beings actually have. It examines poems, myths, prayers, rituals, divination and more.

The author's first novel, *Doing Time*, reflects his years as a chaplain in a Southern US women's prison. It expresses how the harsh reality of domestic violence is the path that leads most women to prison.

Jack's second novel, *No Good Deed* (Wings ePress), is a story which examines America's two great passions: religion and war—revealing how the former can be as destructive as the latter, and how each is glossed with a patriotic morality which hides their darker realities. It follows two friends from the 1960s to the 2000s, one of whom (Kyle) serves in Vietnam while the other (Jon) goes to Canada as a conscientious objector. Their friendship is tested, but unbroken, by their choices. Over time, both become ministers, yet for very different reasons. The institutional church proves to be as challenging as the Vietnam War in ways they could never have imagined.

The author's third novel, **Criminal** *Justice* (Wings ePress), reprieves one of the main characters (a prison chaplain, Stephen Travis) from Jack's first novel, *Doing Time*.

Jack is married to Chris, a former mental health specialist who worked with children and families in the UK. They now reside in France.

Works from the Pen of
Jack N. Lawson

<u>No Good Deed</u> - A Vietnam veteran seeks to find peace within himself, first as a circus clown and later as an ordained minister. Events in his church conspire to reignite his PTSD.

<u>Criminal</u> <u>Justice</u> - A prison chaplain uncovers criminal victimization of inmates by the staff and must decide to risk his job/life for the sake of justice.

<u>The Woods</u> - Life in an enchanted retirement community opens the residents to their deeper selves—for mirth or madness, good or ill.

<u>Dirty Business</u> - An animal scientist uncovers the deliberate dumping of toxic waste, but the notoriety opens the door to further intrigue, danger and murder.